THE SEVENTH TAKING

A MOUNTAIN MYSTERY

BY

BJ BOURG

WWW.BJBOURG.COM

TITLES BY BJ BOURG

LONDON CARTER MYSTERY SERIES

James 516
Proving Grounds
Silent Trigger
Bullet Drop
Elevation
Blood Rise

CLINT WOLF MYSTERY SERIES

But Not Forgotten
But Not Forgiven
But Not Forsaken
But Not Forever
But Not For Naught
But Not Forbidden
But Not Forlorn
But Not Formidable
But Not For Love
But Not Forborne
But Not Forewarned
But Not Foreboding
But Not Forespoken
But Not For Blood
But Not Foreknown
But Not Fortuitous
But Not For Fear
But Not Foreseen

THE SEVENTH TAKING
A Mystery Novel by BJ Bourg
Originally published by Amber Quill Press
April 5, 2015

PUBLISHED IN THE UNITED STATES OF AMERICA

Dedicated to Brandon and Grace: Thanks for standing by me through everything. Your loyalty and support will never be forgotten.

Love, Dad

CHAPTER 1

Mathport, Louisiana
July

"I hate my dad." Joy Vincent pushed a tuft of black hair away from her sticky forehead.

"What'd he do this time?" I didn't really care, but felt compelled to ask.

"I told him I didn't want—" Joy slapped violently at a mosquito that had landed on her arm. "Gosh! Summer just started and these bloodsuckers are already out in full force."

I laughed. "They're not called the Louisiana state bird for nothing."

Joy grunted. "We're going to catch the West Nile virus out here. Anyway, when I told him I was quitting band, he freaked out. Told me I was grounded, that if I didn't do band camp I wasn't doing anything—that I couldn't go anywhere this summer. I'm seventeen freaking years old...he can't ground me anymore!"

Although it was dark, the moonlight cast an eerie glow around the small clearing in the trees, and I could see Joy's bottom lip jutting out like it did when she was angry.

"Aren't y'all leaving for the Blue Summit Mountains tomorrow?"

"First thing in the morning. Before sunrise."

"But I thought you couldn't go anywhere this summer?"

"I can't, but he can, and he's dragging us with him. Trust me— I'd rather stay here than go to that awful place. Did you know there's no cell service in the mountains? None! I won't be able to text you for a week."

Joy walked to where I sat on the old log and I slid over to make room for her.

"You're quitting band?" I asked.

She sighed. "What's the point? You won't be playing football anymore, so I—"

"That doesn't mean you have to quit. Stick with it. I stuck with football, even though I don't have a chance at college ball. You have a real shot to earn a band scholarship at LSU. You're *that* good! Don't quit now. Don't throw all of that hard work away. You've only got one more year of high school. Finish it."

"I'd throw anything away for you." Joy wrapped her arm around my neck and kissed my cheek softly. She moved to kiss my mouth, but I stood up and her arm fell from my shoulder.

"You shouldn't do anything for me. My dad always says you should never make a life-altering decision for a girl—or, in your case, a guy."

Joy waved her hand dismissively. "He's old. Who cares what he says? I love you and I'd do anything for you."

"But you wouldn't be quitting for me—I don't want you to quit. Band is your life."

"If I stay in band, I won't have another Friday night free until Christmas. The same thing with Saturdays. I'll never get to see you when you come in from college."

I couldn't keep still. Sweat beads formed on my forehead, and I didn't know if it was from the smothering heat or my nerves. I walked from one edge of the clearing to the other, swatting at mosquitoes as I did. "I don't want you to quit band. I'd feel bad."

Even in the dim light I could see Joy's brow furrow. She stood slowly, and I could tell she was on to me. "What's going on, Abe? Why'd you want to meet me out here tonight? You saw me earlier today, so I know it's not because you want to see me one more time before I leave. Something's up."

We'd been meeting at that spot since she was a freshman, a few times each month. It was exactly two hundred and ten paces from her window to the clearing and five hundred and four paces from mine. She had to walk through an open field to get there, and I had to push through wild blackberry bushes and anthills. I never cared. It was exciting and fun—except for our very first time. I had been so nervous I'd nearly vomited. I grunted at the memory. It felt like that first time all over again and I thought I would lose my dinner.

"Tell me what's going on," Joy said. "I know you...something's up."

I hesitated, licked my lips. "I...um...I need to tell you something."

Joy tilted her head, folded her arms across her chest. Her eyes looked like dark holes against the pale backdrop of her face. "What?"

I shoved my fists deep into my jeans pockets. "I'll be in college next year, you know?"

"Yeah. So?"

"Well, I kind of wanted to take it easy—enjoy myself."

Joy's face relaxed into a smile. "That's it? God, I thought it was something serious. I want to take it easy, too, spend more time together. I'm sure my dad will eventually give in and let me quit band, and we'll have a lot of—"

"I want to be single."

Joy's mouth opened slowly and then closed, but no words materialized. Her smile faded. She tried several times to speak, but without success. After several long seconds, she finally managed to say, "Wait...*single?*"

I swallowed and dropped my head. "I want to have fun in college. Want to be single."

Her face seemed to fade to a brighter shade of pale. "Have fun? What does that even mean? We have fun. We laugh and joke all of the time. Wait a minute...is this a joke? It is, isn't it?"

I shook my head. "I'm so sorry. I'm just not feeling it anymore. I want to branch out a little, you know? Like maybe date other people or something. Well, not date anyone, but go on dates. Just live free and single for a while."

Tears began to form at the corners of her eyes and glistened in the moonlight. "You're breaking up with me?"

"Look, I'm going off to Southeastern this year and you'll be going off to LSU next year. Pretty soon, we won't even see each other any—"

"You're not kidding! You're serious, aren't you?" Joy dropped to her knees on the rough dirt and buried her face in her hands. "No!" she screamed. "You can't do this to me!"

I glanced over my shoulder in the direction of her house. "Don't be so loud. If your dad hears us, we're dead."

Joy was bawling now. She began gasping for air. I immediately dropped beside her, taking her into my arms for what I knew would be the last time.

"It'll be okay," I whispered.

Joy pulled away from me and slammed a fist against my chest. "How can you do this to me? You said you loved me! I thought you'd ask me to marry you when I graduated!"

My jaw dropped. "I don't want to get married! I'm too young for that real life crap. I want to go to college and have fun, do law school, start a practice. I told you I was never getting married, that I didn't believe in the institution of marriage. I said it more than once. I don't want to get married and I don't want kids and—"

"I thought you'd change your mind. I thought you loved me!"

"I do love you. I love you like a friend."

"Like a *friend?*" Joy gasped. "Oh my God, I can't believe I stayed for you."

I could hardly understand Joy, so I squatted beside her and put a hand on her shoulder. "What did you say about staying?"

Joy looked up. The tears were shiny streaks on her face. "You're the only reason I stayed here."

"What do you mean?"

"My aunt in Birmingham knows how overbearing my dad can be, and she wanted me to go live with her, but I stayed here because of you."

"Your dad was going to agree to this?"

"He didn't know."

I scrunched my face. "You were going to run away?"

Joy only nodded. Her head was down and she was crying. I felt uncomfortable and wanted to leave before I changed my mind out of pity.

"What time are y'all leaving again?" I asked.

Joy said nothing.

"Don't you have to get some sleep? Isn't it like a twelve-hour drive? I don't want you to be tired when you get there."

Joy leapt to her feet and pushed her face close to mine. "Stop acting like you care! You just broke up with me, so it's none of your business what time I'm getting up or how long I'll be in the car or if I'm tired!"

Before I could say anything, Joy spun and ran off in the direction of her house. I sighed and headed home. I'd wrestled with this decision for weeks. I wanted to be single, but I didn't want to upset Joy. We had started out as good friends and I wanted us to stay that way, even though we weren't dating. "Oh well," I said aloud. "I guess that won't happen now."

When I reached the window to my room, I pushed it open and then listened for a few seconds. No movement from inside. I grabbed the windowsill with both hands and squatted, pausing long enough to gauge the distance. At six feet and one inch tall, I had to be careful not to plant my head through the top of the window frame. I took a deep breath. Pushing off with my legs, while pulling with my arms, I propelled myself through the opening. I landed on my bed and rolled to the floor, as though I'd done it a million times before. Out of habit, I pulled the window shut and straightened the curtains—just in case my parents had heard something.

As I changed for the night, my mind was on Joy and the good times we'd had. I slipped into bed and closed my eyes, trying to push her from my thoughts, but all I could see was her sad, tear-streaked face. I opened my eyes and stared up into the darkness. I bolted up and grabbed my phone from the nightstand to make sure it was charged. I sighed, rolled onto my back and tossed it on the bed beside me. I didn't have to worry about that anymore—Joy wouldn't be texting me. Those days of texting deep into the night were gone forever.

My heart started to pound in my chest. I felt a wave of panic wash over me as I wondered if I'd made the right decision. What if I couldn't find another girlfriend? What if Joy found another boyfriend right away? What if it bothered me? My dad once told me I should never break up with a girl if it would bother me to see her with someone else. Yesterday I was certain I wouldn't be bothered, but I wasn't so sure anymore.

I shook my head to clear it, then closed my eyes. As hard as I tried, I couldn't stop thinking about her and worrying if I'd made the wrong choice. I snatched up my phone, tapped the screen to wake it up. I slid the screen over to unlock it and scrolled through my contacts until I found Joy's number. I held my thumb over her name, hesitating. Earlier that day I'd been sure I wanted to be single and I'd called Joy with confidence and asked her to meet me at our spot. Another wave of doubt came over me as I realized we would never be meeting at our spot again and—

"Crap!" I threw my phone into the air and nearly jumped out of my skin when it screamed to life. *Joy?* I scrambled across the carpeted floor on my hands and knees, fumbling around in the dark until I found my phone. My heart raced. I turned it until I could see the screen. I grunted when I saw the name. I inhaled and exhaled forcefully, pressed the button to answer it. "Hey, Charlie, what's up?"

"You don't sound happy to hear from me," said my best friend.

"I was expecting someone else."

"What?" Charlie's voice was shrill. "You didn't break up with her yet?"

"No, I did."

Charlie was quiet for a few seconds. "Dude, you did the right thing. She's a high school kid and you're a college man now—it'd be creepy. Besides, you're supposed to have fun in college, not play house. You're going to meet so many girls next year you won't even remember her name."

"Whose name?"

Charlie laughed. "That's the spirit! You'll get to live like the great Charles Rickman. I can flirt with any girl I want and not worry about getting slapped in the face. Now that I have you on my side, we'll be unstoppable. You'll own Southeastern, and I'll take care of the women back home and then when you get back, we'll—"

"She cried."

"What?"

"Joy...she cried when I broke up with her." I strolled back to my bed and sat on the edge. "I feel like crap for breaking her heart. It would've been easier if we'd been arguing or something."

"Why didn't you start an argument before breaking up with her? Rule number one...before you break up with your girl, get her good and mad so it'll seem like her idea. That way, you're always the victim and the other girls will feel sorry for you."

"I felt bad enough. Maybe I should've waited until she graduated high school."

"And be a prisoner during the best year of your life? No way! Look, it's not fair to stay with someone if you don't want to be with them. Not fair to you and not fair to her."

"I guess you're right." I scrunched my nose when I realized I was taking relationship advice from Charlie. "How do you know so much about relationships when you've never even had a girlfriend?"

"I read *Cosmo*."

I laughed. "Why'd you call anyway?"

"Brett's mom came over earlier to drop off my mom's makeup—she's some kind of a makeup delivery lady or something—and I got to talking to him while they were doing their lady stuff."

"Brett Lester? That transfer kid from Arkansas?"

"Yeah. He's actually pretty cool. He's never seen an alligator, so I told him we might take him camping this weekend and let him catch one."

"Sounds fun. It's been a while since we've gone swamping."

"It might help take your mind off your new relationship status."

*   *   *

It was Saturday morning—a little after daybreak—when we

walked around the last bend in the trail and I pointed up ahead. "That's Alligator Hole."

Brett's eyes were wide. He was as tall as I was and looked like he could hold his own, but he acted scary. "Are alligators dangerous?"

"That depends," Charlie said.

"On what?" Brett wanted to know.

"On how fast you can run. You see, Abe and I don't have to outrun the alligator—we only have to outrun you."

Brett stopped walking. We turned to face him. He stared from me to Charlie, as though searching for a hint of a smile on either of our faces. There was none.

"Wait...you guys are serious!"

Charlie started laughing out loud. He sauntered over and reached up to slap Brett's shoulder. "No, we're not serious. They can be dangerous, but we know what we're doing. You're perfectly safe with us."

It was funny to see a five-foot bag of bones reassuring the giant mountain kid from Arkansas.

"We rule the land," I said, "but they rule the water, so don't fall in."

We had just turned to finish our trek to Alligator Hole when my cell phone rang.

"Don't answer if it's Joy," Charlie said.

"She couldn't call if she wanted to. They don't have cell service in the mountains." I pulled the phone from my jean pocket and answered when I saw who it was. "Hey, Dad, we're almost there. What's up?"

"Abraham, you need to come back home right away." His voice sounded strained.

"Why?" I asked. "We're like fifty yards away. Brett really wants to see an alligator."

"Just get home as quick as you can."

Charlie mouthed the words, "What's wrong?"

I shrugged my shoulders. "Can't I come home after we're done? I'm serious...we're like right there."

My dad was quiet, and I began to worry.

"What is it, Dad? What's wrong? Did someone die?"

"It's...um...it's Joy."

"Joy? What do you mean?" My heart started to thump a little harder against my sternum.

"Son, I'm sorry, but she's missing. They think she ran away and now she's lost."

"Ran away? What do you mean? Where'd she go?"

"They don't know. She got into an argument with her dad while they were hiking in the mountains and she stormed off. They thought she was just walking ahead of them, going to the trailhead, but they never caught up to her. They got all the way to the car and never saw her again."

I slowly sank to my knees, guilt stabbing at my chest. This was my fault. She'd said it herself—*You're the only reason I stayed here.* "Did they look for her? I mean, she has to be somewhere. She can't just disappear. They need to call the cops or something. Get a helicopter. Or dogs. Don't they use bloodhounds to find people who're missing?"

"Abe, they're doing all they can. They've been looking since Tuesday, but—"

"*Tuesday?* She's been missing since Tuesday and they're just now calling us?"

"Son, the last thing on Mr. Vincent's mind is filling us in on Joy's case."

"We have to go to Tennessee!"

There was a long pause. Finally, Dad said, "I'd love nothing more than to go out there to help them, but I can't. I've used up all of my vacation time already. Besides, they have forest rangers trained for this kind of thing. If anyone can find her, it's them. I doubt we could contribute—"

"If you can't go, at least let me. I want to go help. I *need* to help!"

"Abe, you know your mom would never allow it."

"Can you talk to her? Convince her to let me go? I'm sure Charlie can come with me. My truck's got new tires. It's running good—you said so yourself. All I need is gas money. We can sleep in a tent—"

"Abraham, stop. There's no way your mom will let you. It'll cause a fight, and you know it."

"Dad, *please!*" I choked back the tears. If anything happened to Joy I would never forgive myself. I had to do something. Had to get her back. Had to make it right.

"I'm sorry, Abe. I really am."

CHAPTER 2

Seven Weeks Later...

"Abraham Wilson, are you listening to me?"

I tossed my rucksack in the back seat of my pickup truck and went over the contents in my mind. Satisfied I hadn't forgotten anything, I bent and grabbed my hiking boots and a smaller bag from the cement driveway and placed them on the floorboard. I slammed the door, looked first at my phone and then at the distant sky. An orange glow was forming in the east. Charlie needed to hurry or we'd be late getting—

"Abraham! I'm talking to you." Mom's voice was shrill.

Startled, I turned. "Wait, what?"

"Don't text while you drive," she repeated.

I nodded.

Mom left her perch on the front steps and lunged forward to squeeze my neck. She didn't let go.

"It's okay, Rose," Dad called. "He'll be fine. He's been running around the swamps since he was four-and-a-half. He can take care of himself in the wilderness."

Mom released her death grip and wiped a stream of tears from her face. "I know, Dudley, but this is the first time he's driven that far on his own, and it's so dangerous out there. I can't help but worry. They still don't know what happened to Joy and what if he gets in some kind of trouble and—"

"That's why God invented cell phones," Dad reasoned. "He'll call often to let us know he's okay."

I stared down at Mom. She was tall for a woman, but not at that moment. She actually seemed almost as short as Charlie. Her shoulders were hunched and her head hung low. It was a pathetic sight. "Would you feel better if we cancelled the trip?" I asked.

Her eyes lit up. "Yeah, I'd love it—"

"Not gonna happen," I said.

Mom punched my arm. "That's not funny, Abe."

Dad chuckled.

I stifled a smile. "I'm sorry for toying with your feelings. You know I have to do this."

Mom nodded her understanding, then folded her arms across her chest. "My little boy has grown up to be a man. I'm worried, but I'm proud of you for doing this."

"I just need to see for myself." Bobbling headlights and the hum of an engine drew my attention to the street. "Mom, please go inside. I don't want Charlie to see you like this."

Dad guided Mom up the steps and into the house. "Call when y'all get to the cabin," he called over his shoulder.

"Hey, Dad."

Dad stopped in the doorway and turned to face me.

"Thanks. I wouldn't be able to live with myself if I didn't at least try to find her."

"Son, you do realize the search has been called off and you'll be on your own, right?"

"I just have to look for myself. I've got to try and make it right, you know? The counselor said it would help me get some closure."

Dad nodded, then followed Mom inside.

When I turned, Charlie had already parked his car at the far corner of our driveway and was dragging his rucksack from the trunk. The passenger side door opened, and Brett Lester stepped out.

"What are you doing here?" I wanted to know.

"He told his mom and dad we were going camping," Charlie explained. "They were so happy he finally made friends that they said it was okay." Charlie threw his bag in the backseat of my truck, and Brett did the same. Charlie walked back to his car and returned with an expensive-looking camera.

"Whoa! Where'd you get that?" I asked.

The mischievous grin I'd come to know formed at the corners of his mouth and spread across his face. "I *borrowed* it from my mom."

I shook my head. "Roughly translated, you stole it."

Charlie shrugged. "I'm spending my inheritance early. Sue me."

I turned and slipped into the driver's seat. Charlie settled in to my right, and Brett squeezed in the back with the gear. I'd begun to back out of the driveway when Charlie leaned forward, pushed back his brown hair and squinted.

"Is that your mom?" he asked.

"Huh?" I hit the brakes and turned. The curtain on the kitchen window was pulled wide, and Mom was standing in her thick green robe, waving like she had when I went off to kindergarten that first day. Even from that distance I could see tears glistening on her face.

"Ha!" Charlie was doubled over in laughter. "She acts like you're leaving for death row."

"My mom's worse than that," Brett said.

I shook my head, backed out, and headed up the street. I asked Charlie, "What'd your mom do?"

"She didn't even wake up when I left. She told me goodbye last night, and we exchanged nods, like two adults."

"Bull," I said. "I bet y'all held each other tight and cried like newborns."

"You know better than that. She's kicking me out when I turn eighteen—you think she cares about this trip?"

"Oh, that's right." I frowned. "You'll turn eighteen before we get back. Do you mean to tell me you're coming back a homeless person?"

"Who said I'm coming back?"

I smirked. "What're you going to do? Grow a beard and become a mountain man?"

"Maybe."

"Maybe become a mountain man, but you'll never grow a beard."

"Hey," Charlie said, "that hurts. Take it back."

I didn't respond as I accelerated into the curve and merged onto Highway Twelve and headed east. Mathport was finally in our rearview mirror. I smashed the reset button on the odometer and held it until it displayed all zeroes. "Six hundred and ninety miles to go."

"You think we'll find her?" Charlie asked.

"I really don't know," I said. "I don't know what we'll find when we get there."

"Is it true her parents and the law gave up?" Brett asked.

I nodded. "They insist she ran away, and they're probably right."

"Dude, I'm sorry."

I waved my hand. "Let's try to stay positive and have fun. We'll stop at her aunt's house in Birmingham first. If she's not there, then I'll start to worry."

"Why didn't you tell her dad about Birmingham?" Charlie asked.

"Would you want someone giving away your location if you ran away?"

"Good point," Charlie acknowledged. "But why didn't you tell your dad about Birmingham?"

"Because he'd tell her dad."

"So," Brett began, "if Joy's in Birmingham, we won't get to go to the Blue Summit Mountains?"

I shook my head.

"Won't your dad be pissed he rented a cabin for nothing?" Brett asked.

"Maybe," I said. "But I think everyone will be so happy to have Joy back that they won't care."

Charlie looked at me, squinted. "If Joy *is* in Birmingham, she won't want to be found."

"You're probably right."

"What will you do?"

I shook my head. "I don't know. I really don't."

*   *   *

Two hours later, we were approaching the Mississippi state line, so Charlie shoved his mom's camera out the window and snapped a picture of the welcome sign.

"You'd better be careful not to drop that camera," I warned. "Your mom will kill you."

He replaced the cover to the camera lens and tucked it under the seat. "I'm not worried."

"What're you taking pictures of anyway?" Brett asked from the back seat.

"The state signs. I want proof I've been there."

Brett chuckled. "Haven't traveled much, have you?"

"My mom doesn't believe in spending money on trivial things like family vacation."

I checked my mirrors for traffic behind me, but there was none. It was Saturday and most normal people were sleeping at this time. The only traffic we'd seen since leaving Slidell was the occasional big rig that would steadily overtake us from behind and pass us. Each time it happened I was tempted to set pace with them, but Dad would kill me if I got a ticket, so I was reluctantly content to trudge along at the snail's pace of sixty-nine miles per hour.

As I drove, the rise and fall of the rolling Mississippi hills threatened to rock me to sleep. The only sound in the cab was Charlie's heavy breathing and an occasional movement from Brett. I thought about turning the radio on, but I'd have to search for a station—

Wait, what?

I jerked my head around and saw Charlie leaning back in his seat...sound asleep. I shook my head. I was not going to struggle to stay awake while he floated around in a fantasyland flirting with beautiful girls and doing God knows what else. An idea occurred to me, and a smile tugged at the corners of my mouth. I glanced in my rearview mirror. No cars in sight. I looked back at Charlie. His mouth was open and a stream of saliva ran from his lip down his face and dangled off his chin. His chest rose and fell in rhythmic fashion. I bit my lip to keep from laughing and waved for Brett to watch and keep quiet. I took a deep breath, smashing the brake pedal as hard as I could.

The front of my truck dipped violently as our speed dropped from sixty-nine to next to nothing, and the rear of my truck slid sideways in the road just a little. Charlie's body lurched forward, but stopped in mid-flight when the seatbelt locked into place. This caused his head to snap forward and downward. His chin bounced off his chest. He screamed like Mom when she'd see a cockroach and clutched at the dashboard, staring wide-eyed. "Oh my God! What happened? Did we wreck?"

Brett and I burst into laughter. I resumed my normal speed. Tears flooded my eyes and made it hard to see the roadway in front of me. "Dude," I said between violent bursts of laughter, "you should've seen your face!"

"God, that was great," Brett said.

Charlie glanced around, dazed. He felt himself for injuries with hands that shook. "I thought we were dead. Why on earth would you do that?"

"You fell asleep, and if I can't sleep, you can't sleep."

"I wasn't sleeping."

"Oh, right. Your eyes were closed, you were dripping drool all over my truck, and you were about to start snoring—but you weren't sleeping."

"I'm serious. I wasn't sleeping."

"Then why were your eyes closed?" Brett challenged.

"I was staring at the back of my eyelids." Charlie stifled a grin. "I saw a mole on my right lid and I was trying to see if it might be skin cancer."

"In the future, leave that to your doctor. In the meantime, work on keeping me and Brett awake." I started laughing again. "You should've really seen your face. It was priceless."

"Laugh now, but y'all better not go to sleep before me—ever."

Brett chuckled and leaned against his bag. "Nothing you do can top that."

CHAPTER 3

When we were about an hour away from Birmingham, I stopped at a little gas station in Tuscaloosa. I stepped out and shot my thumb at the pump. "One of y'all want to pump while I pay?"

"I'm allergic to fumes." Brett rearranged our bags and stretched out on the backseat. "Wake me when we get there."

"I've got it." Charlie walked around the truck and grabbed the handle of the hose. "You want me to drive the rest of the way?"

"Yeah, that'd be nice. I can hardly keep my eyes open." I walked inside the convenience store and paid for eighty bucks of gas. When I walked back outside I slipped into the passenger's seat and winced when my knees hit the dashboard. Charlie stuck his head in the driver's door, allowing the fuel to pump.

"You okay?" he asked.

"Yeah, I keep forgetting just how short you are."

"I'm not short," he said. "You're just a freak. Your legs are stilts."

I grabbed the release button beside the seat and tried to slide it all the way back, but it snagged on something.

"Hey, get off me," Brett protested.

"Move to the other side. Charlie's so short you'll be able to fit a small elephant back there." When Brett was clear, I reclined as far as it would go, pulled my seatbelt on, and closed my eyes.

"Want something to drink before we leave?" Charlie asked.

I shook my head, not opening my eyes.

"I'm going to sleep, too," Brett said.

"Losers. I'll be right back."

My body relaxed into the seat. It felt good to let my eyelids close after so many hours of forcing them open. I jerked when I heard a distant click, and recognized it as the automatic shut-off of the pump. I shifted in my seat and started to block out my surroundings. I wondered how close to a full tank eighty bucks had gotten us and if we'd have enough money to get back home or if I'd have to call my parents for more. The sounds of passing cars, slamming doors, honking horns, and people hollering—all normal city sounds—started to fade to a low drone.

I found myself wondering what I'd be doing right then if I hadn't broken up with Joy. Would we be sitting back at home somewhere taking it easy? I was certain she wouldn't have run away. What if she hadn't run away? What if she was in trouble? What if she was…dead?

I shuddered and dismissed the thought.

The driver's door slammed and broke through my thoughts. The truck rocked slightly as Charlie entered and settled into his seat. The engine hummed to life. Cold air soon blew through the vents. Using my right arm as a pillow, I leaned against the window and exhaled long and slow. I felt the smooth lurch as the truck began to pull away—

"Holy crap!" Charlie screamed.

I jerked up, wide-eyed. "What happened? What's going on?"

Brett was staring wildly about, his eyes half open. "What was that noise?"

I stopped short, then shook my head. "I'm not buying it. You're trying to get us back for earlier."

Charlie threw the gearshift in Park and stepped out. I heard someone yelling and turned to see the owner running toward us.

"Why did you do that?" the owner yelled, pointing at the side of my truck.

I hurried out and ran around to the driver's side. I gasped when I saw the gasoline hose hanging from the hole in my truck. It had been ripped from the pump.

"You've got to be kidding me," I said.

Charlie frowned. "I don't know how I forgot to put it back."

Brett was bent in half, laughing like a hyena.

"Six hundred dollars," the owner said. "You'll pay me six hundred dollars or I'll call the police!"

"Chill out, old dude. No need to call five-o." Charlie dug money out of his pocket, rifled through the bills, then turned to me. "I need four hundred more."

"No," I said. "That'll wipe us out. Let him call the cops."

The owner shook his finger at Charlie and said, "You'll be arrested."

"Are you kidding?" I asked. "It was an accident."

"You'll pay me six hundred dollars or you'll both go to jail," the owner said.

"I'm using my college money for this trip, and I'm not giving you a dime. Call the cops." I turned to walk away.

Charlie grabbed my arm. "Dude, if I go to jail, we're definitely not finding Joy. Look, it'll be fine. Just give him the money so we can get out of here and go find Joy."

I crossed my arms, shaking my head. "Charlie, if we give him all our money, we're done. We'll have to go back home. We won't be able to afford gas money, let alone food."

Charlie leaned close. "Dude, I've got this. Trust me."

"But I need to find Joy. I can't go back without at least trying to find her."

"It'll be fine, Abe." His voice was a whisper. "I've got a backup plan. We've got all the money we need. *Trust* me."

Suspicious, but curious, I dug the money from my wallet and reluctantly handed it over. "You'd better know what you're doing."

Charlie winked and handed the money to the owner. "No cops?"

The owner pocketed the money, retrieved the broken hose, and waved us off. "Go away! Don't come back."

I slipped into the passenger's seat, and Charlie got behind the wheel.

"This trip is over," I said. "You and I gave him all our money and this loser"—I shot my thumb back at Brett—"doesn't have a cent to his name."

"No, it's not over." Charlie started the truck and tossed something in my lap.

I glanced down and saw a credit card.

"The limit's five thousand dollars," Charlie said triumphantly. "We're set."

As Charlie drove out of Tuscaloosa for the second time, I lifted the credit card and studied it. "Where'd you get a five-thousand-dollar credit card?"

"I found it when I broke into my mom's safe."

"You're a thief?" Brett wanted to know.

"She doesn't know you have it?" I asked.

"Nope and nope."

I dropped the card as though it were a bomb. "You are a thief! And we're going to jail as accomplices."

"It's in my name, so it's mine. I didn't steal anything."

"But you stole it from your mom's safe." I thought about that for a second. "Wait a minute—what's your mom doing with a credit card in your name?"

"That's what I'd like to know. I guess she needed the money. Who knows? In any case, she's the thief, not me. She stole my identity."

I put the credit card on the center console. "How'd you break into the safe?"

"Picked the lock with two paperclips."

"You're crazy." I shook my head. "What were you doing in her safe in the first place?"

"I wanted a copy of my dad's birth certificate and death certificate." Charlie drove in silence for a long minute. "I wanted to start doing the ancestry thing. Find out who I really am."

I never knew what to say when Charlie mentioned his dad, so I did the usual—kept my mouth shut.

"How'd your dad die?" Brett asked.

"None of your business," I blurted out.

*   *   *

"This is the street," I told Charlie. "Joy's aunt lives in the second to last house on the right."

Brett whistled when we turned into the driveway. "I see why Joy wanted to live here."

The house was perched on a large tract of land that housed at least a dozen fine horses. I stepped out of my truck on shaky legs. "Y'all wait here."

"You sure you don't want us coming with you?" Charlie asked.

I swallowed, then shook my head. "I messed this up, so now I have to fix it."

"Suit yourself." Charlie pushed the driver's seat back hard, laughing when Brett called out in pain.

As I walked up the long cement driveway, I scanned every window at the front of the house. I half expected to see Joy peering through the curtains as I approached the large wooden porch, but that didn't happen. What happened instead was that the main door flung open and a robust woman pushed through the screen and stood staring at me with beady eyes.

I stopped abruptly. "Um...hello, ma'am. I'm Abraham—"

"I know exactly who you are, boy. What are you doing on my property?"

I wiped my sticky hands on my shirt. "Um...I was hoping Joy

was here."

The woman's eyes narrowed and her face reddened. "Is this some kind of sick joke? Were you not satisfied enough crushing her poor heart that you have to come here and harass me?"

I raised my hands. "Ma'am, you don't understand. She told me I was the only reason she didn't run away to your house, and when I found out she'd disappeared, I thought she might've come here to—"

"I understand perfectly. You're a cold-hearted kid who likes to string young ladies along until you're done with them. At that point, you discard them like a pair of used socks and move on to your next victim. Get off of my property before I call the law!"

"But is she here?"

"Boy, she disappeared in the mountains—you should know that by now. They gave up the search last week. Found no evidence she was even there."

"I know. They think she ran away because she was fighting with her dad." I swallowed and summoned the courage to ask again, "Is she here? Did she run away to here?"

The woman's eyes remained cold, but tears stamped out the blue of her eyes like dark clouds blotting out the sun. "For all we know she's dead—and it's all your fault! Get the hell off my land before I call my husband out here to give you the beating you deserve."

I stood frozen. *What now?* I was certain she was here.

"Leave now, young man!"

I nodded, turned on my heel and hurried back to the truck. Brett was in the front passenger's seat, but I didn't waste time telling him to move. I slipped into the back seat and slapped the headrest behind Charlie. "Go! She's not here."

Charlie's mouth opened wide. "What now? What do we do?"

I pursed my lips. "Now we go to the mountains and we look for her."

*   *   *

I didn't say much during the rest of the trip. I tried to sleep to drown out the guilt, but it was no use. My chest ached. I figured I was too young to have a heart attack, otherwise I would've made Charlie drive me straight to the nearest emergency room—it hurt that bad.

When we finally arrived in the mountains, Brett used the roadmap to guide Charlie to the Bear Mountain Cabin Rental building. It was a cabin-looking structure directly off the main strip—a tourist-packed street that sliced through the mountain. Once Charlie had parked, we entered the lobby. An elderly lady with large-rimmed glasses looked up from the counter and smiled. "Can I help you guys?"

"Abraham Wilson," I said. "We have reservations for the Squirrel Nest cabin."

"Ah, yes." She pulled a large yellow envelope from under the counter, then dug out a set of keys with a plastic card attached to the ring and handed it to me. "Here's the key to your cabin. This card will allow access to four of our clubhouses on the mountain. They're open from nine in the morning until ten at night and have swimming pools, hot tubs, game rooms, and snack machines." She handed me a map of Bear Mountain and showed me how to get to the cabin.

I thanked the lady and took the map and keys. Once in my truck, I backed out of the tiny parking lot and we made our way carefully along the narrow mountain road. It must have only been a mile or two to the cabin, but the winding road made it feel like fifteen. When we finally arrived at the cabin, I stopped in the driveway and shut off the engine.

The rustic cabin was a lot bigger than it looked online, which was nice. The deadbolt stuck a little and I had to wriggle the key to unlock it. Brett pushed by me when I finally got it open, and Charlie and I followed him inside. We found ourselves in a dining room and kitchen combination. Just beyond the kitchen was a large living room furnished with a sofa, loveseat, recliner, and a giant flat screen television. The entire right side wall of the living room was glass.

While Charlie explored the cabin, I grabbed my phone to call Mom. She answered midway through the first ring.

"Abraham, are you okay?"

"We made it."

"Thank God," she said.

"Is Dad around?"

"Yeah," Mom said. "He's right here."

Dad got on the phone and asked about the drive.

"It was great," I said. "The scenery was cool, and the cabin's awesome."

"That's good." There was a long pause before he said, "Promise me you'll be extra careful out there."

"I will." I paused for a few seconds. "I'm really scared, Dad."

"I know, Abe. Look, the only reason I agreed to help pay for your trip was so you could see for yourself that she's gone and move on with your life. Please don't let this consume you. We agreed to one week—"

"I know, I know. If I don't find her in one week, I'm heading back home."

"Right. You have to think about getting ready for college. I know it's hard, but when we lose someone we have to keep going—we have to move on."

"It's the not knowing that kills me."

"I know, son. Whatever you do, please don't blame yourself anymore." I didn't respond, and Dad finally asked, "When are y'all going out to the spot?"

"First thing in the morning," I said. "We'll try to spend nine or ten hours a day searching. We should be back at the cabin before nightfall each night."

"Alright, just be careful." As was his custom, Dad hung up without saying goodbye.

I turned to Charlie and Brett. "I appreciate y'all coming with me. I couldn't do it alone."

Charlie walked up and gave me a half-hug. "That's what friends are for."

Brett nodded. "It's cool."

I took a deep breath, then glanced around the cabin. "We start looking first thing tomorrow, but nothing says we can't unwind tonight. Why don't we find something to do to take our minds off of everything?"

"Like what?" Charlie asked.

"Let's go check out one of the clubhouses before they close…see if the Tennessee girls are as hot as the Alabama girls," Brett suggested.

"Sounds like a plan," I said.

CHAPTER 4

When I pulled into the driveway of the cabin, I caught my breath. The truck shook as Brett and Charlie scrambled out of the bed. They jerked the passenger's side back door open and squeezed through the opening at the same time, grunting the entire while. Once they were crammed into the seat, they slammed it shut. Their breathing was heavy. I thought I heard teeth chattering.

Charlie punched my shoulder hard. "Dude, you could've gotten us killed—and all for your precious seat covers!"

"Holy crap," was all I said.

A black bear was pawing at the metal bear-proof garbage receptacle at the edge of the driveway. He was near the front door of our cabin. When the door had slammed, he'd turned his head and stared at my truck for a few seconds. He was about ten feet from us, but I could tell his back was easily as tall as the hood of my truck—and he was on all fours. If he were to stand on his hind legs he would be taller than the top of my truck.

"You think it'll attack?" I asked.

"I sure hope not," Charlie said. "He looks like he could flip your truck over."

I studied the area. "How will we get inside the cabin?"

"I don't know. I'm not making a run for it." Charlie shoved Brett hard. "Get out there, Arkansas. See if it attacks you."

Even in the deep shadows of the approaching Blue Summit Mountain nightfall, I could see Brett shaking. "Uh-uh...I'm not leaving this truck!"

"Neither am I," I said. "I read where a bear can run, climb, and swim better than any human being alive."

"Well, if it comes down to it, I don't have to outrun the bear, just y'all," Charlie said.

"Too bad for you I work out on a regular basis," I countered.

"Too bad for you I'm all skin and bones. That bear would take one look at me and decide I'm not worth the effort. But you"— Charlie gave a confident nod—"you're big enough to feed on for at least two or three days."

I didn't like this talk about a bear chewing on me, so I changed the subject. "You think that bear's big enough to drag someone away and eat every bit of them?"

"Ah, I see where you're going with this." Charlie was thoughtful. "I don't think so."

"Wait—what did I miss?" Brett asked. "Where're we going?"

"Look how big he is. He's got to be able to snatch up a small-framed person and carry them away," I said.

Charlie frowned. "But not without a trace. That bear would have to use those giant teeth to grab his victim and that would leave a lot of blood in the area."

"You're right." I sighed. "If a bear got Joy, there would've been blood and they would've found something."

The bear finally turned back toward the metal receptacle and continued grabbing at it with its huge paws. When he couldn't get the door open, he pushed his stomach up against it, wrapped his arms around it, and began pulling on it.

"Holy bear crap," Charlie yelled. "He's about to pull that thing out of the ground."

He was right. The receptacle swayed back and forth and was in danger of being ripped from the metal brackets that held it to the concrete driveway. Thinking back to everything I'd read about bears while trying to figure out what had happened to Joy, I remembered seeing something about park rangers using fireworks to scare bears away from cabins. Loud noises, I thought, glancing around the truck. When my eyes settled on the steering wheel, I punched the horn and held it down. The noise that emanated from under my hood was not as impressive as I first thought it would sound, but it had the desired effect. The bear jerked backward, releasing the receptacle, and nearly fell on his haunches. He twisted away from us and sprinted into the forest in a rambling type motion.

"He doesn't look so fast." Charlie eased the truck door open. "You got the key, hero?"

I nodded.

"Ready?" he asked.

"Y'all really think it's a good idea?" Brett wanted to know.

I grabbed the door handle with my left hand and held the key in my right hand. "Do you want to wait until it comes back?"

"I guess not." Brett licked his lips.

"On three," Charlie said. "One…two…*three!*"

We all jumped out of the truck, pushed the doors closed behind us, and raced toward the cabin. I fumbled with the key, trying desperately to fit it into the keyhole.

"Hurry," Brett said. "I don't want to die!"

"I'm trying." After much wriggling of the handle, the key finally slipped into the hole, and I pushed through the opening. We fell inside, and I kicked the door shut behind us, reached up and threw the deadbolt. "Phew! That was close."

"What if we encounter bears on our hike?" Brett asked.

I walked to the living room, dug through my bag, and brought back a can of bear spray. "I came prepared."

Brett shook his head. "Did it look like mace would work on that big monster?"

I frowned. He did have a point. "I don't even think an elephant gun would drop that evil beast."

"Seriously, Abe…what if we run into that giant demon out there on the trail? We won't have a cabin or a truck to hide in. If he decides to charge us, we're dead." Brett crossed his arms. "You said yourself that the forest rangers looked everywhere for Joy. If they couldn't find her, what makes you think we can?"

"You having second thoughts?" I asked.

"Shut up, Brett," Charlie said. "I don't know how y'all do things in Arkansas, but we Louisiana boys stick together."

I thought back to the stories I'd read about the few people who had been mauled and killed by bears in recent times in the Blue Summit Mountains. I reminded them of the attacks and turned to Brett. "Look; I can't ask you to come if you don't want to. I guess it *will* be a little dangerous. I'll totally understand if you don't want to come along, but it's something I've got to do. I can't just leave Joy out there alone. You can stay here if you—"

Charlie waved me off. "We're not splitting up. There's strength in numbers, and we don't know what we'll find once we hit the woods. Besides, the people who got attacked were all camping in the back country and most of them were attacked in their tents at night. We're going out in the morning and getting back before dark. We ain't sleeping in no tents. We'll be fine."

Brett wasn't so sure. "You remember telling us about those two people who got mauled last year? That was in broad daylight."

"Those don't count," Charlie said. "That one man got too close to the cub and that kid was walking around with food in his hand. They were just stupid."

"I guess so." Brett was thoughtful. "The size of that bear shocked me. I'm not ashamed to admit it scared the crap out of me. I imaged they were a lot smaller—like the size of a Rottweiler or something."

"Me, too. I didn't realize they got so big around here. You don't have to come if you don't want—seriously. No hard feelings." I walked to the refrigerator and opened it. Nothing. I searched through the cabinets. Same. "There's no food in here."

"Want to eat some stew?" Charlie asked. "I've got a couple of cans in my bag."

I pointed to the door. "It's out there with the bear."

Brett shook his head. "I don't know about you guys, but I'm suddenly not hungry anymore."

"Neither am I. In fact, I'm still full from earlier." I glanced around the cabin. "Which room do y'all want?"

"Whichever one doesn't have a window," Brett said.

"I'm sure they all have windows." I entered the room adjacent to the kitchen area and looked around. "I'm pretty sure this is the honeymoon suite."

Charlie followed me and laughed when he saw the heart-shaped tub next to the heart-shaped bed with the heart-shaped pillows. "Brett gets this room."

"That's fine." Brett dove onto the giant heart. "I'll take it."

There was a door leading out onto a back porch, so I opened it. I found a light switch and flipped it on, lighting up the deck. I took a careful step outside, scanning the area for bears before I fully committed to leaving the doorway. I made my way to the railing and peered over the side. The glow from the light wasn't strong enough to penetrate the darkness of the thick trees, and I couldn't see the mountainside below. Large posts were the only things holding up that side of the deck. "You think that bear can climb up those posts?"

"I don't know," Charlie said. "He was pretty fat, so I doubt he could drag his big butt up here. As long as we make sure the doors are locked Brett should be okay."

I turned to look at him. "What about you?"

"I'm sleeping up in that loft, where I know he can't get to me."

Suddenly, there was a loud snap somewhere beneath the deck. My heart skipped in my chest. Charlie's eyes widened.

"Was that the bear?" Charlie asked.

"I don't know." I leaned over the railing, straining to see the base of the posts, but it was no use. More branches snapped as whatever it was moved slowly away from the cabin and deeper into the forest. Within minutes, cicadas began their deafening death rattle and we could no longer hear the rustling in the bushes. When we were sure it was gone, we returned inside the cabin, and Charlie made his way up to the loft while Brett settled into the honeymoon suite. That left me sleeping on the couch. It was leather and I started to sweat within minutes, but at least it was soft.

*   *   *

I woke up the next morning to the sound of zippers and snaps and things being tossed around. I opened one eye and looked toward the sound. Charlie sat at the small dining room table, the contents of his rucksack scattered on the floor.

"What're you doing?" I asked.

Charlie looked up. "Lightening my load. I'm only keeping enough food for today, since we're coming back to the cabin tonight."

"Good idea." I tossed the blanket off and stretched. Dragging my tired frame off the sofa, I walked outside and scanned the area before approaching my truck. Keeping my head on a swivel, I grabbed my bags and hurried back into the cabin. I tossed them onto the sofa and dumped everything out. I shoved enough food for one day, a bottle of water, my fork, and the length of rope I'd brought along. I shoved my small bag into the rucksack and turned to Charlie, "Do we need matches for the hike?"

"No. It's not like we're sleeping out there in the wilderness." He walked to the honeymoon suite and shoved the door open. "You coming or not?"

Brett walked out with his bag slung over one shoulder. "I wouldn't miss it for anything."

I nodded my thanks, as I tossed the box of matches aside. After I was done with my rucksack, we stepped out onto the shady driveway in front of the cabin. It was a lot cooler than I expected, considering it was the middle of summer. Keeping a cautious eye on the thick forest surrounding us, I pulled the cabin door shut and locked it. There was no sign of the giant bear from the night before.

"Let's saddle up," I said, and we climbed into my truck.

With Charlie playing navigator, we made our way off Bear Mountain and drove for what seemed like forever on the road leading to Tipton Bluff, which marked the beginning of our hike.

"How far is it to the Tipton Bluff Road?" Brett asked.

Charlie consulted the map. "We have to be close—about three miles."

"Three miles left to go?" I asked.

"Looks like it," Charlie said.

I wanted to drive a little faster, but the sharp curves wouldn't allow it. Before long, the road curved ninety-degrees to the left and then whipped around to the right near an area a sign called the Newfound Gap. It was a large parking lot with stairs leading up to an overlook. There were about four cars in the parking lot, but we didn't see any people. I kept driving and soon came to a sign that directed me to veer right onto a narrower road, surrounded on either side by thick forests. Another sign indicated it was seven miles to Tipton Bluff. As we traveled along this road, we came upon a number of pullouts that provided awesome views of ridges and valleys. We stopped at a few of them to snap some pictures, but made good time along what we had come to realize was a typical mountain road.

"Look." Charlie pointed. "There it is."

I strained to see where he was pointing, but all I saw were trees. "I don't see anything."

"Look at the top of the tree line. You see it?"

I shook my head.

"I do," Brett said.

Charlie stabbed his finger repeatedly in the air. "That giant piece of rock sticking out above the trees. It's the bluffs."

"I still don't see it." It was difficult picking something out of the faraway tree line while trying to keep from crashing into the jagged mountainside. "I'm trying not to kill us."

"I appreciate that more than you know. Just drive. I'll take a picture for you." Charlie leaned out of the window and snapped some pictures.

Before long, the road widened to the left and the trees on the right gave way to a jagged rock wall. The two lanes were soon divided by a grassy median and it opened up into a large parking lot. The grass in the median was manicured, and there were a number of small trees growing at various locations along it. There weren't many cars in the parking lot, and we were grateful to get a parking place close to the beginning of the trail. I took a spot to the left that overlooked an expansive range of mountains and valleys. We stepped out and, as though in a trance, walked to the sidewalk and found ourselves standing at what appeared to be the edge of the world, staring out at mountain upon rolling mountain for as far as our eyes could see. The mountains closest to us were dark green. As they extended away from us, they faded into a light gray and blended in with the blue skyline. In the distance, we could see a river cutting its way through one of the valleys.

"Is that one of the rivers on the map?" Charlie asked, referring to three crooked fingers of rivers on our map that extended from the southernmost part of the trails we would be hiking.

"I don't think so," I said. "I think those rivers are on the other side, nearer the Cherokee Trail."

Brett shook his head. "Arkansas doesn't have mountains like this."

"Really?" Charlie snapped more pictures and then turned to me, a solemn look on his face. "You ready to do this, Abe?"

I nodded, before I returned to my truck and pulled out my rucksack. Charlie stuffed the camera in his pack and then looked over at Brett and me. "Are y'all going to put on the hiking boots?"

Brett shook his head and retrieved his bag.

I thought about it for a few seconds, while I considered pulling them on. I was wearing a pair of leather water shoes that were a lot more comfortable than my hiking boots. "I don't think so," I said. "We'll hike to where she was last seen and search all the trails in the area first. I read that's what the rangers do when someone goes missing, so we'll follow that plan. Tomorrow, we'll branch out into the wilderness and go deeper and deeper each day."

"Sounds good. I won't wear mine either." Charlie walked around to my side of the truck and leaned against the bed, wiping his face.

I glanced down at his water shoes and squinted when I saw flashes of silver on each shoe. There were about five of them. "Why do you have safety pins on your shoes?"

"The straps broke," Charlie said.

Brett started laughing. "Um, why not buy new shoes? They're like twenty bucks. If one of those pins pop off you'll be walking barefooted."

"Stop worrying about my shoes and grab your stuff." Charlie walked away from us and stopped at a large monument-looking display case and the entrance to the trailhead.

I shrugged into my rucksack, locked up my truck, and Brett and I joined Charlie by the display case.

Charlie turned to us, his face a shade whiter than I was used to seeing. "This ain't good at all!"

We flanked Charlie and looked up. Protected behind the glass of the display case was a giant map of the Blue Summit Mountains. Taped to the outside of the glass was a picture of Joy, along with a message asking anyone with information about her disappearance to call the park rangers. But that wasn't what had caused Charlie's concern—it was the other six posters taped to the glass. My heart pounded in my chest as I scanned the faces and read the details.

"So...Joy's not the only one?" Brett's voice shook.

"Joy's the seventh person to go missing from this area since 2006." Charlie stabbed at each of the posters with a finger and read off the locations of each disappearance. "Oliver's Bald, Eagle's Gap, Tipton Bluffs Bypass, Rocky Ridge Trail, Rocky Creek Trail, and Betham Creek Trail—we're headed right into the heart of that area."

I studied the map. Charlie was right. We had to pass nearly every disappearance site to get to where Joy went missing. Realization finally came to me. "She didn't run away—she was taken!"

Brett threw up his hands. "I'm out! I didn't sign up for this. I was willing to go out there looking for a girl who got lost, but this looks more like Big Foot is eating people."

"Not just people," Charlie corrected. "Young adults—they were all between fifteen and twenty when they went missing. Four girls and two boys."

"Holy crap!" I nearly vomited when I noticed the dates of all the disappearances. "They all went missing in June!"

"Joy went missing in June. This is eerie."

I looked over my shoulder, scanning the area. A few tourists were walking to and from the parking lot and a couple of park rangers stood huddled near an old wooden structure drinking something in deep mugs. When I was sure they weren't looking, I quickly ripped all of the posters down, then slung my rucksack off my shoulders.

"What're you doing?" Brett asked. "You're going to get us in trouble."

"There might be a link between what happened to Joy and what happened to these people." I folded the posters and shoved them into the large pouch of my bag, where they would be safe. "We'll need this to help find Joy."

"You're not serious?" Brett asked. "After all of this you still want to go out there?"

"We're not in danger," I said. "It's the end of August. No one has ever disappeared during the month of—"

"Look here!" Charlie moved next to me and showed me a news article on his phone. "The law called all of those disappearances suicides."

"Even Joy's?" I asked.

Charlie shook his head. "It's from last September, long before her deal. But it talks about the six kids in those posters."

I snatched the phone from his hand. The caption read, 6 Kids, 6 Years, Month 6 since '06—Coincidence or Curse? "They're calling this a curse or a suicide? Which is it?"

Charlie leaned over my shoulder and scrolled down through the details, stopping on a paragraph. "Here—some of the locals thought these kids were cursed because nearly one hundred people went missing from 2006 through 2011 and all were found except for them. They thought it might have been some sort of ritualistic thing."

I read over the article. "So, every other person who went missing was found?"

"Right," Charlie acknowledged, "every single one of them. Of course, they weren't all found alive. Somewhere in the article it says a small percentage of the people who go missing in the mountains die, but it's rare they go missing without a trace. In fact, in the last hundred years, only six people have never been found—well, seven now, counting Joy."

Brett was pacing like a caged animal. "So, is this place cursed or not?"

"Some locals think the curse was broken, because the devil—or whoever they think it is—got his six sacrifices." Charlie started to chuckle when he saw the look on Brett's face. "But you can calm down. They think the curse was broken because no one disappeared last year."

"So, it was cursed, but now it's not?" Brett's face twisted in confusion.

"That's what the superstitious types think," Charlie explained. "The cops say all of the kids were having problems in their lives and went off into the wilderness to die alone. They called it 'returned to nature' or something corny. They say it's something kids do nowadays—like a suicide trend."

Charlie was right. Some top park ranger was quoted as saying the only difference between the six kids who were never found and the hundreds of people they've recovered over the years was trouble at home. I couldn't breathe. I felt weak. I leaned against the display case and slid down until my butt hit the ground. "It's my fault. She ran off because I broke up with her. She said I was the only reason—"

Charlie quickly squatted beside me. "First off, she ran off because she was fighting with her dad, and that had nothing to do with you. Second, we don't know for sure that's why she disappeared. But if they *are* right, she's still out there and it's up to us to find her. Everyone else has given up."

"But didn't the cops search for like eight weeks?" Brett asked. "That's longer than most search and rescue missions in the mountains. If the park rangers didn't find her, we definitely won't be able to. We shouldn't be doing this. We need to get out—"

"How hard do you think they searched once they realized she was fighting with her dad? And that her boyfriend had broken up with her the day before they left?" Charlie shook his head. "Once grownups form an opinion about something, nothing can change their minds. Joy's still out there, and we need to find her."

I took a deep breath and struggled to my feet. "Charlie's right. No matter what, she's still out there. Even if she's... Even if she died, we need to bring her back home."

Brett shook his head. "This is a bad idea. I don't like it one bit. I'm not going."

"Would you want us going home if you were stranded out in the wilderness?" Charlie asked.

Brett shrugged. "I wouldn't be stupid enough to run off into the mountains like an idiot. She should've known better."

My blood instantly boiled. I jerked the truck keys out of my pocket and flung them at Brett. The keys ricocheted off his chest and fell to the paved parking lot. "If you don't want to come," I shouted, "get your ass in the truck and stay there! I'm sick of your whining. You knew what we were doing, so why'd you even come along if you're such a coward?"

"Easy, Abe." Charlie turned toward the park rangers—they had stopped talking to look our way. Smiling big, Charlie waved. They stared for several long seconds and then resumed their discussion. "Phew! That was close."

I turned back to Brett. Tears had formed at the corners of his eyes. He chewed on his lower lip, and I knew he was trying to maintain his composure. No boy likes to cry in front of his friends. To save him the embarrassment, I shouldered my bag and walked off, Charlie beside me.

CHAPTER 5

Charlie and I walked in silence up the steep narrow trail for about twenty minutes. It was a blacktop path and the walking was smooth, but the trail was much steeper than I'd anticipated.

Charlie finally broke the silence. "Don't worry about him. He's not one of us, anyway."

"I should've kept my cool. I can't blame him for being scared. Hell, I'm scared, too. We don't know what we're doing out here—what we'll find."

"But you don't hear us crying about it. Real men—"

"What about real men?" a voice called from behind us.

Charlie and I spun to see Brett standing there, face covered in sweat, breath coming in gasps.

"What do you want?" Charlie asked.

"I'm in," Brett said.

Charlie's eyes turned to slits. "For real this time?"

Brett nodded. "For real."

"No more complaining?" Charlie asked.

Brett shook his head.

I smiled, walked over and slapped Brett's back. "Sorry for losing my cool."

He nodded his acceptance of my apology, and we turned to continue up the trail.

When we had rounded a blind curve in the trail for about the tenth time and the end still wasn't in sight, I asked, "It's two miles to the top?"

Charlie nodded. "That's what the brochure said."

"It's pretty steep." I took a deep breath, but it felt hollow. My lungs starved for the thick bayou air I was accustomed to. "It feels like we've walked ten miles."

"This is the steepest thing I've ever been on," Brett said. "I've hiked in the Ozarks a lot and don't remember a mountain ever being this steep."

"Are we going to have to hear about your Ozark Mountains all week?" Charlie wanted to know.

Brett laughed. "Am I going to have to look at those ugly shoes the entire trip?"

"These ugly shoes will kick your butt."

We hadn't gone much farther before we reached a wooden bench off to the right. There was a lady and a small girl sitting on it. They were both breathing hard and appeared exhausted.

"Are y'all coming or going?" Charlie asked them.

The lady took a deep breath and blew it out. Sweat dripped down her forehead and her long blonde hair stuck to her rosy cheeks. "We're on our way down."

The small girl was pouting and leaning against the lady. "I want to go home," she said.

We smiled at her and continued up the path. On the right side of the trail the mountain extended upward into the sky, with trees protruding from the rocky ground. I wondered how a tree could grow out of solid rock. To the left, the ground was blanketed with thick, chest-high grass that stretched away from the trail for several yards before dropping off gradually and merging with the crowded forest. The trees seemed to be growing on top of each other and appeared to be a great hiding place for wild animals. Pretty soon, I knew, we would be leaving this paved trail and plunging into the depths of the Blue Summit Mountain wilderness.

I didn't want Brett to know it, but I was scared. If we met up with a giant bear that had bad intentions, we were dead. We were no match for the likes of what we'd seen outside our cabin. And the fact so many people our age had disappeared forever caused my stomach to turn. I kept telling myself we were okay because it wasn't June anymore.

"Hey, there it is," Brett said, pointing to a faded wooden sign along the trail.

The Cherokee Trail was nothing more than a faint dirt path that cut a narrow swath through the deepest and most desolate portion of the Blue Summit Mountain National Forest. We paused by the trailhead, traded glances, and then plunged along. We had walked barely a mile when a downed tree obstructed the path up ahead. I pointed to it. "Let's stop by that roadblock. There's something I want to show y'all."

"What is it?" Charlie asked.

"You'll see." I continued toward the obstruction, carefully scanning the army of pine and oak trees surrounding us. A bear could be anywhere. I'd read that there were over two thousand of them out there—and they all had to eat. I waved my hand around. "There could be a bear behind every tree."

"Yeah," Brett said from behind me. "I'd feel much better if the can of bear spray wasn't stuffed in our backpacks, out of reach."

When we reached the downed tree, we shrugged our packs off and rested them side-by-side on the rough bark. Although the tree was firmly on its side, it was as high as my waist. Heeding Brett's advice, I unzipped my small bag and dug out my can of bear spray, then shoved it into the right side pocket of my cargo shorts. Charlie dug out his, but stuffed it into the front of his waistband. "I don't want my can getting tangled in the flap of my pocket," he said. "You might want to do the same."

"What about me?" Brett asked. "Do I get a can?"

"Did you pack underwear and a toothbrush?" Charlie wanted to know. "Or was I supposed to bring that for you, too?"

I dug in one of the smaller pouches. When I felt the cold blade of the knife I'd made for Charlie, I smiled. "Close your eyes, Charlie."

He eyed me with suspicion. "Why?"

"So I can punch you in the face without you seeing me." I shook my head. "Just close your eyes and hold out your hands."

Frowning, Charlie obeyed my command. I pulled the knife from my bag and placed it into his hands, careful not to lop off a finger. "Okay, open your eyes."

Charlie opened his eyes, slowly at first, and then they widened. "What is it?"

"Be careful. It's really called a push dagger, but I prefer to call it a punch dagger," I said. "It's six inches of pure punching evil."

Charlie made a fist around the handle of the knife and let the six-inch blade extend between his ring and middle fingers. "Wow, this is a mean-looking blade. Did you make it with your bench grinder?"

I nodded. "If a bear comes at you, just punch it right in his chest."

"That's insane," Brett said.

Charlie threw a couple of wild punches into the air with the knife and then executed a clumsy uppercut to the underside of an imaginary bear's jaw. "You think the bears are scared of me now?"

"I don't know, but they'll definitely be scared of Jezebel." I reached deeper into my bag.

Charlie stopped admiring his knife and looked up at me. "I didn't know you had a new girlfriend."

I pulled out the knife I'd been working on nonstop for nearly two months—ever since the moment I'd found out about Joy. It had helped me stay busy and kept my mind off the bad thoughts I was having.

"Holy smoke, that's cool." Brett reached out a finger to touch the edge of the blade, but I pulled it back.

"It's razor sharp." It was a double-bladed knife with the handle positioned in the middle. I'd paid twenty bucks for a piece of 440C stainless steel from a knife-making store out of Texas that I'd found online. The original piece of steel was twelve inches long, a quarter of an inch thick, and two inches wide. I had begun by cutting a four-inch handle from the center of the steel and then I shaped out identical blades on either side, each of them four inches in length. I'd taken my time on this knife, shaping the blades and polishing them to perfection. I knew I would need it.

"You call it Jezebel?" Charlie asked.

"Yep."

"Why?"

"It just sounds evil," I said. "Like that woman in the Bible."

Brett looked from Charlie to me, frowned. "Do I get a knife?"

"I don't think so." Charlie was still staring in awe at my blade. "You might hurt yourself."

"I can stab straight up or down and slash upward or downward with it, all without changing my grip." I scanned the area, spotted a tree about twenty yards behind us. I waved for Charlie and Brett to stand beside me. I grabbed one of the blades and lifted the knife to my ear. After setting my feet, I threw Jezebel with all of my power. She shot through the air, tumbling end over end, and came to rest with a solid thump in the tree. The blade vibrated solidly in place. We jogged over, and Charlie whistled when he saw how deep she had embedded into the tree.

"That's scary," he said.

I had to wriggle Jezebel for several seconds before I could free her from the grips of the tree. "I could probably kill a bear with this."

"No kidding." Charlie nodded in agreement. "How far can you throw it?"

"But what about me?" Brett asked. "Do I get a knife?"

Ignoring Brett, I said, "I can probably throw it fifty yards, but I can only make it stick consistently at twenty-five, thirty yards."

Charlie suddenly frowned. "How're you going to carry it without stabbing yourself?"

I dug in my bag and pulled out a makeshift sheath that I'd fashioned from an old leather belt I'd found in the attic. It was one of my dad's old belts from when he was a kid, and it was wider than any belt I'd ever seen. The sheath extended from my belt down the right side of my leg and was solid except for an opening where the handle was located. I secured the knife in the sheath by pushing one of the blades upward into the top slot, sliding the other blade into the bottom slot, which was open at the front, and snapping it in place with a leather strap. "Like this," I said, after it was in place.

"Nice." Charlie held up the punch dagger I'd made for him. "What about this one?"

I dug deeper into my small pack and found a sheath I'd made for his knife. "It straps to your belt and the knife shoves straight down into it."

Charlie took it and immediately slid it onto his belt. "Dude, I really appreciate this. It's the coolest thing anybody's ever given me."

"That's because I'm the coolest person you know."

"No," Charlie said. "I'm the coolest person I know."

"What am I?" Brett wanted to know. "Bear bait?"

I smiled, fished a butterfly knife out of my bag, and tossed it to him. "You can have this one. My dad bought it for me as a Christmas present two years ago."

Brett's eyes widened. "This is awesome! I've never held one in real life."

"Don't cut your fingers off." I turned away as they admired their blades. My mind was off down the trail, wondering what we would find. I pulled out the posters and studied them. The first disappearance site—the one that started it all—was a bit up the trail. Jillian Wagner had been a nineteen-year-old from South Carolina. One day she'd had her whole life ahead of her, and the next day she was gone—disappeared into thin air. I stared at the dark shadows around us and shuddered. We needed to get this done so we could get out of the mountains before dark.

I pulled my rucksack back on and waved for Charlie and Brett to saddle up. They did, and we scrambled over the downed tree and continued down the narrow path. According to the poster, we'd have to walk two miles to get to the place Jillian vanished. I counted my steps so we would know when we got close to it.

The smell of pine clung to the cool morning air as we walked.

We didn't talk much, but when we did, it was in whispered tones. I don't know why—it's not like there were people around. When we weren't talking, the only sound we could hear was the muffled crunch of our shoes against the bed of needles that coated the ground beneath us.

I had paced off about a mile when we heard a branch snap off to the right of the trail. We all stopped immediately. I turned to look at Charlie and Brett, who'd crept up close to me.

"You think that was a bear?" Brett asked.

I shook my head, as I strained to penetrate the shadows of the dense forest with my eyes. Another branch snapped, and I thought I saw a dark shadow move somewhere in the distance. "Keep walking," I whispered.

We picked up the pace. I stared constantly toward the right, but didn't hear the sound again. After pacing off another mile, I raised my hand, and we slowed to a stop. "This is two miles," I said. "It should be right around here."

There was a large rock beside the trail, and Charlie dropped his rucksack onto it. "This has to be the spot."

"Yeah, I doubt there're two trees like this." It was a large pine and it looked like it had grown right up through the rock. The roots stretched like gnarled fingers from under the rock and extended across the trail. "How could that happen? How does a tree grow right through a solid rock?"

"I don't know, but this is definitely the spot." Charlie grabbed the camera from his bag and snapped a picture of the tree.

After I dropped my rucksack beside Charlie's bag, I pulled out the map I had downloaded at home. I also read the poster that detailed Jillian Wagner's disappearance and compared it to our surroundings. It was spot on. "Okay, according to Jillian Wagner's boyfriend, she was last seen walking off the trail near this rock. She went off to relieve herself, but never returned."

Charlie moved about twenty yards down the trail and looked back to where I stood. "The boyfriend walked about this far and then waited. Why would he do that? Why wouldn't he go with her?"

"First off, no girl wants her boyfriend standing over her while she's peeing. Second, he told the park rangers he wanted to make sure no one came up the trail while she was peeing." I paused, looked around. Something seemed odd. Birds chirped, leaves rustled, and tree branches groaned above us, but there were no other signs or sounds of life. No movement whatsoever. It dawned on me then. "Hey, did you realize we haven't seen a person since leaving the

Tipton Bluff Trail?"

Brett, who had wandered off the trail to throw rocks in a creek, turned and looked back toward me. He suddenly didn't like that there was a distance of twenty yards between us. He quickly retraced his steps and stood beside me, scanning our surroundings. "It's kind of eerie out here."

"I know." I pointed deeper into the forest behind the rocky tree and asked Charlie, "How far do you think Jillian went off to use the bathroom?"

"You mean the tree."

"What about the tree?" I asked, confused.

"There're no bathrooms out here, so she had to use a tree," Charlie said.

"Whatever." I set off into the forest at a ninety-degree angle to the trail. I realized Brett was so close to me I could almost hear his heart beating. I kept looking behind us toward Charlie until I reached a point in the forest where I was sure I couldn't be seen from the trail. "She must've been at least this far, so she couldn't be seen from the trail."

We walked around the area, searching for—what, exactly? Dozens of searchers had combed this mountainside seven years ago searching for any sign of Jillian, and they had turned up nothing. The ground was mostly covered in oak leaves and pine needles, with a smattering of green leafy plants, and if the search party had missed anything, it was buried under six years of leaves and needles. I squatted against a tree and surveyed my surroundings, imagining I was a nineteen-year-old girl all alone in that particular area.

"What happened to you, Jillian?" I asked out loud. If I could figure out a link between these six strangers and Joy, it might lead me to her—or to what happened to her.

"What do we know about this girl?" Charlie had joined me and Brett.

I glanced at the poster, refreshing my memory. "She was from a small town in South Carolina, had wrapped up her second year of high school, and was on vacation with her boyfriend of two years."

"Oh, I remember reading about her in that article. Some of her family suspected foul play." Charlie pulled out his phone, held it up, and walked around.

"No reception?" Brett wanted to know.

"Nope, but I think of everything," Charlie said, his chest rising with pride. "I took screen shots of the article." After fiddling with his phone for a while, he nodded. "Yeah, they suspected her boyfriend,

Ted. He was three years older than her, and her family thought she'd found a new boyfriend in high school and he found out about it."

"They think he killed her?" I asked.

"He denied it, but they did accuse him of killing her," Charlie mumbled as he read. "Nope, it wasn't him. He took a polygraph and passed."

"You think the polygraph can be beaten?" I asked Charlie.

He shrugged. "I suppose."

"Holy crap," Brett blurted out. "I know what he did!"

Charlie and I both turned to him. He just stood there smiling.

"Well?" I asked.

"The boyfriend killed her somewhere else and hid the body really well, then came out here to the mountains and made up a story about her going missing. If they're looking for her here, they won't be looking where her body really is."

"That could work." I nodded, liking it. "That would explain them not finding her body."

"Except he passed the polygraph," Charlie reminded us.

"Right, there is that." I stood and walked in an ever-widening circle, trying to penetrate the needles and leaves with my eyes. "There must've been something. Some sign she was here. They had to have missed it. People don't just vanish into thin air."

"Unless she was abducted by a UFO," Charlie said. He began taking pictures of the area, as though he were a detective on a crime scene.

"Keep talking like that," I said, "and you'll find yourself in a straightjacket, with a side of electrotherapy."

"They'll have to catch me first." Charlie pointed to something white on the ground. It was partially obscured by some leaves. "What's that?"

I picked up a small stick, bent close, and moved the leaves away. A rancid smell immediately rose up and gagged me. I jumped back and tossed the stick down. "Are you kidding me?"

"What is it?" Brett tried to see around me.

"Someone took a crap out here and left the dirty toilet paper behind." I kicked some pine needles and leaves over the stained toilet paper and turned away. "They must've not read the article on toilet use."

Charlie chuckled. "I don't blame them. I wouldn't want to carry my own crap around for hours until I found a garbage can. I mean, where would I keep it? Brett's pocket?"

"They don't expect you to carry your crap in your pocket," I said.

"The pamphlet says to bury feces in a six-inch hole and pack out any toilet paper you use."

"You see, Charles, you don't have to carry out your smelly crap—only your crap-covered toilet paper."

"You'll be needing toilet paper to pick up the crap I kick out of you if you call me Charles again."

I moved back toward Cherokee Trail. "Let's head to the next site. I think if we hurry we can get there within the hour."

"Isn't it two miles?"

I nodded. "It's near that camp called Oliver's Bald."

Charlie shut off his phone. "I hope we don't need nine-one-one for anything."

I thought I detected a hint of uncertainty in his voice and was suddenly questioning our decision to be out here. We had traversed miles and miles of swampland back home, but we had always had cell service. We had always been one phone call away from rescue if we ever got in trouble, and that was always a soothing thought. But out here, we were on our own. Completely. And we were moving deeper into the wilderness and farther away from civilization.

CHAPTER 6

We returned to the hybrid rock-tree and continued on the Cherokee Trail. None of us said much as we walked, as the enormity of the situation started to set in. Sure, it was only a day hike, but the rough ground, steep cliffs, and raging rivers could turn on us at any moment. One wrong move on the uneven ground and we could become instantly incapacitated. Even if only one of us got hurt, we'd be screwed. Two of us might be able to carry the other for a ways on a normal day, but I doubted we could go a hundred yards without stopping over this rough trail. If one of us did get hurt, it would take too long to hump out of here and we'd end up stuck out here at night. I shuddered at the thought and changed the subject in my mind. I decided to focus on counting my paces so I would know when we reached the next disappearance site.

We made decent time ascending and descending the mountain trail—walking over downed trees and occasionally stubbing our toes on protruding rocks. When I had paced off almost two miles, we saw a splintered stick with two wooden slats attached to it that marked a fork in the trail. The slat that was parallel to our path had "Cherokee Trail" and an arrow pointing straight ahead carved roughly into the faded wood. The other slat pointed toward our left and had "Oliver Ridge Trail" carved into it. The slats had seen better days and some of the letters were chipped away, making the name of the trail almost impossible to read. Had we not studied our maps, it would've been easy to take a wrong turn.

"We're supposed to take Oliver Ridge Trail, right?" Charlie asked.

"Yep. Looks like it's a half mile to Oliver's Bald." I stuffed the map into the back pocket of my cargo shorts and shifted my rucksack. While it wasn't very heavy, it was starting to pull on my shoulders and the muscles in my neck ached. The back of my shirt was also starting to feel sticky. Although it wasn't very hot on the shadowy trail, I was sweating.

We turned onto the Oliver Ridge Trail and immediately felt smothered. The trail was nothing more than a foot-wide patch of packed earth that cut through the thick grass and trees like a slender snake. It was too narrow to walk side-by-side, so I took the lead. The grass on the edges of the trail tickled my legs as I walked and made them itch. Occasionally, I had to turn my shoulders sideways to fit between encroaching trees on either side of the path, and my rucksack snagged on the branches two or three times, forcing me to lurch forward in order to wrench it free.

"You sure this is right?" Brett asked.

"You saw the same sign we saw." Charlie's voice came from some distance behind us.

"I know, but I can't imagine anyone actually walking along this trail," Brett said.

A low-lying tree limb loomed ahead. When I reached it, I had to squat at an awkward angle to pass under it without bumping the top of my rucksack. "I guess that's why they call this the back country."

"You know if a bear attacks us we're dead," Brett said. "We're like a mouse in a trap."

"I doubt a bear could fit in here." I had to step around and dip under so many trees that it was difficult to count my paces. "I'm not sure how far we've come."

"We should see the shelter through the trees before we get to it," Charlie said.

"What happened up there?" Brett asked. "Who disappeared?"

"Some seventeen-year-old kid from Detroit named Dave Burke," Charlie said. "The missing person poster described him as a ghost hunter wannabe—or was that the other guy? Anyway, he should've been a magician because he just disappeared into thin air."

I slowed to step around a leaning tree and felt something slam into my back.

"Sorry about that," Brett said.

I paused and turned to look at him. "You feel okay?"

Brett looked around, then turned back to me. "You know, this sounded like a good idea while we were back in Louisiana, but now I'm not so sure."

I nodded my understanding and looked past Brett at Charlie, who was bringing up the rear. "Charlie, you do realize Dave Burke disappeared along this trail while lagging behind his friend, right?"

Charlie scoffed. "I ain't worried."

I smiled when I saw him shoot a quick glance over his shoulder and quicken his step. I remembered reading that Dave's friend said he was within eyesight of the shelter at Oliver's Bald when he turned around and realized Dave was gone. That had been two years earlier, on June 23, 2011, and he was the last one to go missing until Joy...

I cringed at the thought of Joy out there all alone. She didn't like the woods as much as I did and bugs scared her. I shook my head. There was no way she ran off to commit suicide through nature. Something happened to her—something bad.

"Why'd we stop?" Brett asked.

I leaned over, waved him past me. "Why don't you go ahead and take the lead for a while."

Brett hesitated, chewing on his bottom lip. "But..."

I reached for my sheath and palmed Jezebel. "I've got the rear—just in case."

Brett nodded his thanks and slipped by me. I waved Charlie on, too. Brett looked back to make sure we were right behind him and then began pushing his way through the gauntlet of hostile branches that struck out at him, and Charlie and I followed. I was vividly aware I was in the same position Dave Burke had been in when he disappeared. Of course, Dave didn't have Jezebel. As I clutched the handle of my knife with whitened knuckles, I wondered if the evil that Dave had encountered on this same desolate path had been a physical being. If not, what good would Jezebel be?

A branch suddenly snapped behind me, and I whipped around, my heart racing. I pointed Jezebel at the sound, flexing my hand over the handle. Had I really heard the noise? Or was my imagination playing tricks on me? "Hey!" My voice was a mere hiss. "Did y'all hear that?"

When they didn't reply, I turned around. They were not there. They'd been swallowed up by the thick forest. My throat tightened. I lunged forward, ignoring the sting of the branches against my face. "Charlie! Brett!" I was yelling now. "Where are y'all?"

"Shush!"

I heard the sound off to my right. I jerked to a stop and peered through the thick trees and underbrush. Charlie was standing several feet to the right of the trail, his back pressed up against a thick oak tree. Brett was beside him and they were staring down the trail, eyes wide. I turned my head slowly and saw a black bear about the size of a large German shepherd. I chuckled. By bear standards, it was a baby.

"What're y'all so freaked out about?" I asked.

"Don't get any closer," Charlie warned. "Where there's a bear cub, there's a mom."

The bear was down on all fours and blocked our passage forward. It didn't seem to notice us as it stared into the forest toward our left. Its rounded ears were perky and its brown snout lifted to the wind, as though trying to decide if it was safe or not. After several seconds of sniffing the air, it gingerly finished crossing the trail and disappeared behind the trees. We waited for at least five minutes, scanning the area carefully in search of solid black fur. Finally, I turned to them.

"Y'all think it's safe to pass now?" I asked.

"How should I know?" Charlie asked.

Still holding onto Jezebel, I stepped forward. "I'm getting out of here, with or without y'all."

"Why don't we just wait a little longer?"

I shook my head and continued walking. "If something wanted to attack us out here, we'd be helpless. It could be on top of us before we even knew what hit us. We'd never see it coming. Besides, I heard something back there, and I don't want to find out what it was."

I didn't need to look back to know Charlie and Brett were right on my heels.

"Yeah," Charlie said. "The sooner we get to the shelter the better."

"I can easily understand how Dave Burke went missing. Heck, I turned for a second earlier, and when I looked back, y'all were gone"—I snapped my fingers—"just that quick."

My burning thigh muscles told me the trail was rising. It curved right, then left and then straightened for a short distance. Just as I reached the end of the straightened portion of trail, I caught sight of sunlight reflecting off a sliver of metal roof. I stopped suddenly and spun around to make sure Charlie and Brett were still there. They were. I sighed. "I can see the shelter through the trees. Dave must've disappeared right around here."

Brett pointed to the shelter. "Let's hurry and get to it before the bear and his momma decide to come back."

I pushed my way through the thick grass and brush at the edge of the trail and entered a small clearing where the shelter was located. The structure was backed up against the mountainside and consisted of a roof, two large tree posts, and a chimney on the right side. I pulled out my map. "This is definitely the shelter at Oliver's Bald."

Charlie moved up beside me. "This is not what I envisioned when I read about this shelter."

"Yeah, I thought it was supposed to be a real cabin," Brett said.

There was a bench fashioned from a felled log under the outer edge of shelter's roof. Centered under the roof was a roughed-out picnic table with two other log benches. Charlie pulled off his rucksack. After tucking Jezebel back in her sheath, I followed his lead. A chill ran over my back when my rucksack fell to the ground and the cool mountain air hit my wet shirt. I reached back and tried to pull the shirt away from my skin. I began to wish I'd brought a change of clothes.

Brett had walked all around the shelter, testing the strength of the support planks. He finally dropped his pack on the picnic table. "You really think people sleep in here?"

"I doubt it," I said. "There's absolutely no protection from wild animals."

We began to look around the shelter and saw a fire ring just outside the covering to the right. There were some blackened and partially burned tree branches at the edges of the ring.

Charlie squatted beside the ring. "These are old."

"Oh, yeah?" I challenged. "How do you know that, mountain man?"

"Because they're cold."

"No joke. We haven't seen a soul all day." I dug through my rucksack and pulled out the posters. I stared at Dave Burke's picture. "Out of all the cases, this'll be our best chance of finding something that will help us solve Joy's case," I said. "He's only been missing two years, so there's a chance we could still find something. Maybe some of his gear, bones…something."

"What—are we detectives now?" Brett wanted to know.

"Two years is a long time." Charlie kicked at the ground and sent a pile of dead leaves flying into the air. "You know how much of this stuff has fallen since last year? If there is anything out here, it's probably buried under all this crap. It'll be like finding a needle in a haystack."

"The Battle of Lafourche Crossing was fought in 1863 and I found a couple of lead bullets under the bridge when I was a kid."

"Yeah, you told me that story before," Charlie said. "At the time, I didn't have the heart to tell you the truth, but I think it's time you learn."

"What're you talking about?"

"Your dad planted those lead balls to make you think you were something special."

"He really did?" Brett asked.

"Whatever." I started to walk off. "Y'all coming or not?"

"I am," Brett said, sticking to me like glue.

They followed me back up the trail to where we thought Dave's friend had stood when he first realized Dave was missing. We searched one side of the trail first and then the other, sifting through the leaves and tall grass, hoping for even the slightest sign of Dave Burke's passing.

At one point, Charlie stopped digging to look up at me. "How do we know if we've dug deeper than one year's worth of leaves?"

Not knowing the answer to that question, I ignored it. "Just keep looking," I said. "If we find something that belonged to him, we'll know it."

"Hey, that article listed all of his property!" Charlie fished his phone out of his pocket and tossed it to me. "Check it out while we dig around."

I caught the phone with one hand and accessed the touch screen. A quick scan of the article proved Charlie right. Dave's mother had provided a long list of gear and personal property he had taken with him. According to the friend, Dave was wearing his backpack at the time of his disappearance and everyone found it strange that the backpack was never recovered.

"Surely," one expert had speculated, "even if wild animals had devoured Mr. Burke's entire body, they certainly would not have eaten the backpack, so we'd have eventually found it. This small detail lends credence to the young man's theory that ghosts and spirits make their homes deep in the Blue Summit Mountains National Forest."

"This was the ghost hunter," I told Charlie. "Some FBI guy said this was a 'hoax perpetrated by two attention-seeking ghost hunters who wanted to garner attention for their cause.'" I scrolled farther through the paragraph. "And then there're those who thought the absence of the backpack proves he meant to return to nature. They say if you don't want to be found out here, you won't be."

"Still doesn't explain the lack of a body," Charlie said from his perch on the ground. "I read in one of those articles that the rangers watch the buzzard activity when someone goes missing. They said it usually leads to the dead person."

Whatever had happened to Dave Burke, we didn't find a shred of evidence telling us he had been here. For that matter, outside of the cold, charred branches in the fire pit, we didn't find a shred of evidence that anyone had been in this area ever.

"Did you really expect to find something?" Charlie asked. "Hundreds of people scoured this very same mountainside looking for Dave. If they couldn't find anything right after the disappearance, we definitely won't find anything two years later."

We looked up and realized we had ventured out of eyesight of the shelter. "We'd better get back before something happens to our gear," Charlie said.

I nodded.

"What could happen?" Brett asked. "You worried a bear might steal your backpack and charge up your credit card?"

We trudged through the thick leaves—sometimes sinking to our ankles in the soft blanket that covered the rough mountain floor, and sometimes tripping over stumps and rocks hidden beneath the vegetation. We eventually returned to the shelter to find our rucksacks on the log benches, undisturbed.

"Want to get moving?" I asked. "We should be able to make it to the spot where Mable Bragg disappeared within the hour and then we can eat lunch."

"Where'd she disappear?" Brett asked.

"Right where this trail intersects with Betham Creek Trail." I scanned our surroundings, swallowed hard. "I can't help but wonder if Joy is out there right now—cold and hungry, waiting for someone to rescue her. What if we find nothing? What if we have to return home empty-handed?"

Charlie slapped my back. "We'll figure it out. For now, let's get out of here. This place really freaks me out. I don't know what it is, but I keep getting the feeling we're being watched."

I slowly scanned the area. "I wonder if that momma bear is out there somewhere stalking us."

"I don't want to stick around to find out." Charlie pulled his rucksack onto his back and set off down the Oliver Ridge Trail without even waiting for us.

"Hold up," Brett said, dipping his shoulders into the harness of his rucksack. "Unless you want to end up like Dave Burke."

"Dave was bringing up the rear, remember?" Charlie called.

Brett quickly caught up to Charlie, then glanced over his shoulder. "Hurry up, Abe. We can't get separated out here."

I shook my head and joined them on the trail. We labored on, and the deeper into the backcountry we traveled, the more strenuous the hike became.

CHAPTER 7

"Where's that Betham Trail?" Charlie asked, without turning around.

I pulled the map out of my pocket and stared at it as I walked. "It should be coming up to the left."

Charlie shook his head. "You said that twenty minutes ago, Abe."

Brett looked from left to right. "Are we lost? Please don't tell me we're lost out here!"

Several minutes earlier we had passed a faded path that broke off to the right and, according to the map, Betham Creek Trail was supposed to be just up ahead. I began to worry we had drifted off the trail. There were a few spots where the path was overgrown from lack of foot traffic and we'd had to venture out at several different angles until we picked the trail up again. "The trail's so faint...I guess it *is* possible we set off on an animal path."

"An animal path?" Brett stopped abruptly, and I almost crashed into him. "You mean we could be walking down a bear path? So, we're completely lost and we're walking straight to certain death!"

"Stop worrying so much." I gave Brett a shove to get him moving again. I hoped my own nervousness didn't bleed through in my voice. With over half a million acres of wilderness surrounding us, we could die of starvation if we ventured off course. "If we don't run up on it within the next few minutes, we'll double back and—"

"Never mind, navigator," Charlie called. "We're there."

I ducked under a collapsed pine tree leaning against an ancient oak and followed Charlie and Brett to the sign pointing toward Betham Creek Trail. It was more worn than the last sign we'd encountered and I wondered if the trail was even more desolate than the Oliver Ridge Trail. The path was wider where the two trails intersected, and we stood staring at the ground.

"Is this the spot?" I asked.

Charlie pulled out his phone and scrolled through the article. "It says Mable Bragg was last seen at the intersection of Betham Creek and Oliver Ridge Trails. This is the intersection."

I frowned. The poor girl had been sixteen when she disappeared—the second youngest of the missing persons. She was a redhead and looked a lot like Charlie's little sister, Tabitha.

"What's the four-one-one on her?" Brett asked.

"Dude, don't ever say 'four-one-one' again." Charlie looked away from Brett and glanced over the article. "Um, let's see…she'd been camping with her mom, dad, two brothers, and some family friends. While the grownups were barbecuing at a campsite twenty yards away, the teenagers decided to play hide-and-seek. Mable was 'it' and stood at the intersection to count to a hundred. The teenagers who were in earshot of Mable said she suddenly stopped counting at sixty-four—"

"At this very intersection?" Brett asked.

I nodded. "It's weird to be standing right where someone disappeared."

"Anyway," Charlie continued, "the other kids were all hunkered down in hiding spots by then and assumed she was coming out early to find them. They'd been hiding for about thirty minutes when they got bored and started coming out one by one to meet at the intersection."

"Mable was gone when they got here," I said.

Charlie nodded. "They figured she'd pulled a fast one on them and was already eating a plateful of barbeque while they were stuffed into uncomfortable positions waiting for nothing to happen. They went back to the campsite, but Mable wasn't there. The rest is history."

"How long did they search for her?" I asked.

"Um…it says hundreds of people searched for several weeks. They don't say exactly how long."

"She was having problems at home?" I asked.

Charlie nodded. "It says they all had some sort of problems at home, which was why the cops thought they all wanted to go missing."

I turned my head and began searching for the campsite. According to the article, it was due south of the intersection and was marked by a metal barbeque pit and a few primitive tables and benches. I walked in that direction and paused, trying to penetrate the shadows of the thick trees. In the distance, I thought I detected some sunlight filtering through the trees. I pointed toward the spot. "That's got to be it."

"Good," Brett said. "I'm hungry."

If there was a trail leading to the tiny clearing, we couldn't find it. Most of the walk was clear of underbrush, but we encountered a thick patch of briars. I pulled out Jezebel. "Stand back."

Charlie and Brett got behind me, and I started chopping at the branches on the briar bushes. Each swipe of the blade only pushed the thick branches and wouldn't slice through them. Because of the thorns, I couldn't grab the branches to hold them in place to cut. I scanned the area. "There's got to be a way around this crap."

I walked around and finally found a lane in the bushes just wide enough for us to slide through sideways. I led the way, moving slowly so as not to get stabbed in the exposed legs by the inch-long thorns on the branches. The briars tugged at my rucksack as I moved, and I had to give an occasional jerk to break free.

"I've never seen pickers this long," Charlie said.

"They're not called pickers here, my little Cajun friend. They're called thorns." I paused to wipe blood from a spot on my right calf when we'd made it to the other end. "I didn't realize I got stuck."

Brett had walked off ahead of us and was standing in the clearing. "You guys, this is an excellent spot to stop."

I strode over to the picnic table made from split logs and shucked my rucksack from my shoulders. As advertised, there was a metal barbecue pit and some benches. The pit was rusted, but appeared solid. It was anchored solidly to the ground. Just beyond the picnic table, a stream flowed by and I headed straight for it. When I reached the stream I stepped out onto one of the rocks. "This is awesome."

Charlie had walked up to the stream's edge. "It's paradise."

The water was crystal clear and wasn't very deep. Maybe two or three feet. The streambed was solid rock, with some of them protruding above the rushing water and some buried beneath. There was a rock jutting above the surface of the water about six feet from where I stood. "You think I can make it?" I asked.

"Don't even try," Charlie warned. "If you get hurt, we're not carrying you all the way out of here."

"Do it," Brett challenged. "If you get hurt, Charlie and I will only have to outrun you—not the bear."

"I'm seventeen, not seventy." I squatted, took a deep breath, and lunged forward, propelling my body through the air. I covered the short distance with no problem and both feet landed on the protruding rock. I was about to give a triumphant shout when my left foot slipped out from under me and shot into the air, sending me flailing backward. I crashed into the stream and sucked air when the freezing water wrapped its icy hands around my body. It was not deep enough to cushion my fall and my back slammed into the uneven rocks. Although I wanted to bolt from the clutches of the biting water, I was temporarily paralyzed from the pain in my back. I groaned.

"I told you," Charlie yelled from the bank of the stream. "Don't listen to me."

The water flowed over my body and splashed in my face. Shivering, I pushed off the slick rocks with my elbows and sat up. My shirt clung to my body. I glanced around. "What happened?"

"Algae grows on these rocks," Charlie said, mocking me, "and it makes the rocks very slippery."

I made my way to my feet and staggered toward the stream bank, where Charlie and Brett stood laughing. My body was so cold that the cool wind blowing against me felt warm. "I wish I'd brought the matches. I'm going to freeze to death."

"It's summer," Charlie said. "You won't freeze to death."

"You could," Brett warned. "It's much cooler up here in the mountains."

I dropped to the ground in the middle of the patch of sunlight that beamed down into the clearing and stretched out on my back. I didn't move, allowing the sun to caress my body with its warm fingers.

"Let's eat so we can get out of here." Brett glanced around. He seemed uneasy.

"I'm with him," Charlie said.

I looked back toward the intersection of the two trails, but couldn't see them because of the dense underbrush and shadows. "Y'all want to go back or keep going?"

"How far have we come?" Charlie asked.

I stuck my hand in my back pocket and grunted when I felt the wet mush that used to be my map. "Dudes, my map's ruined."

"Good job, Abe." Charlie dug his map out and handed it to me. "Why don't you try not to ruin this one, okay? It's all we've got."

I spread it out and studied it. "We've already traveled ten miles, so that means we have seven to go."

"Let's keep going then," Charlie said. "Besides, I'd rather not go back to Oliver's Bald. That place gave me the creeps."

"Me, too!" Brett said. "Do we even have to come back this way, or can we get back to the truck from another direction?"

"There is another way, but from what I read, Rocky Creek Trail is narrow and the going might be slower." I handed the map back to Charlie and dug for some food.

We broke open a can of beef stew and shared it, along with a bottle of water. Although cold, the beef stew was tasty and hit the spot. I hadn't realized how hungry I was until I smelled the food. With each bite, my energy level increased until I felt like I could hike another ten miles with little effort.

Charlie finished eating before Brett and me, and he stood with the camera. He took a picture of me wolfing down my last bite and then shot pictures of the surrounding area. "I sure wish we knew what happened to Joy—and these other people," Charlie said out loud, but not particularly to me.

Brett nodded, as he wiped brown gravy off his chin with a sleeve. "It's got to be scary out here for days or months alone."

Guilt stabbed at my chest, just as it had done when Dad first told me Joy was missing. Without saying a word, I gathered up our trash and put it in a nearby metal trash receptacle. I absently wondered how they'd gotten the receptacle all the way out there in the backcountry.

"You think she's dead?" Brett asked.

I took a deep breath, then exhaled slowly. "I sure hope not. I pray not. I feel bad enough as it is."

"Oh, I'm sorry, Abe. I didn't mean—"

I waved it off. "It's okay. We're all wondering the same things and thinking the worst. Regardless of what happens, I do sincerely appreciate y'all coming with me. I couldn't do this alone. It is scary, but y'all make it manageable."

"Can we hug it out?" Charlie asked, trying to stifle a grin.

I couldn't help but laugh. He could always lighten up the mood.

"I wouldn't hug you if I was dying of hypothermia," Brett said.

Charlie stuffed the camera in his rucksack and slung it over his shoulder. "What do y'all think happened to them? You think this place could be haunted by ghosts?"

"Ghosts don't exist," I said.

"According to the news article, they all had issues at home that could've been grounds for them wanting to run away"—Charlie nodded in my direction—"even Joy."

I shook my head. "Lose the suicide angle. I don't think Joy could ever hurt herself."

"I'm not talking about suicide. What if they wanted to disappear?

Joy was always smart—straight As, all honor classes, top of the band. A smart girl like that doesn't go wandering off to be lost forever." Charlie moved closer, and I saw he was getting excited, like he did when he thought he had a prized alligator on the other end of his line. "If a girl like that wants to disappear, she plans it carefully. How much you want to bet she did a little research before leaving for Gatlinburg and saw that people were going missing? How much you—"

"You're right!" I was nearly jumping with excitement. "She planned this. The article said it's been a year since anyone disappeared, so there's no way her disappearance is connected. I bet her aunt is in on it. I bet her aunt met her here and picked her up."

"She's probably hiding out in a hotel or something in Birmingham," Charlie said.

I nodded. "She knew her aunt's house would be the first place her dad would look, so there's no way she was going there. Did you notice the way her aunt was acting? Like she was hiding something."

"She looked pissed off to me," Brett said.

"Whatever, dude. It doesn't even matter anymore. Charlie's right. She ran away, and her aunt helped her." I walked over and slapped Charlie hard on the shoulder. "You're brilliant!"

"I know; I know."

"If you're so brilliant," Brett said, "why don't you solve the case of these other missing people while we're here?"

Charlie stood a little taller. "I might just do that."

"If Joy ran away, what did happen to the others?" Brett asked.

I shrugged my shoulders. "Maybe they ran away, too. Maybe they snuck out of the mountains and moved to some small town where they're living in peace—away from their controlling parents. And maybe they committed suicide by nature, like the park rangers think."

"I'm not buying it," Brett said. "We all have problems, but we don't disappear to die, and we don't run away from home over some small fight. I think their suicide theory is an excuse for their incompetence. Think about it—if you sucked at your job, would you admit it? Or would you blame the kids who went missing? If you think about it, we can all come up with some bogus reason why we'd want to run away from home and disappear."

I glanced over at Charlie. "He does have a point. If we go missing, people would probably say you disappeared because your mom's kicking you out the house when you turn eighteen, and they'd probably say I wasn't happy about going to college."

"You see," Brett said. "They'd say that I was mad about my mom forcing me to move to Louisiana after she divorced my dad. They'd say I'm hitchhiking my way back to Arkansas."

I laughed, as I looked over at Charlie. My smile faded when I wondered what might be going on inside his head. He stood like a statue and was staring down at the ground, his T-shirt and cargo shorts swaying gently in the cool breeze. When he looked up, his eyes were different. It was as though he were looking through me instead of at me. "Did y'all ever think of disappearing? Starting over in a place where no one knows you? Like witness protection?"

I gulped. He was serious. "Um, not really. I mean, I remember wanting to run away as a kid when I'd get mad at my mom and dad, but I never acted on it. Within a day or two, I'd always get over whatever it was that made me mad."

"For the last four years, all I wanted to do was finish high school, but now all I want to do is go back." Charlie grunted. "If I could go back to that first day of freshman year and relive the last four years, I'd do it in a heartbeat."

"Come on, Charlie...we've been dreaming about this forever. We've talked about what we'd do when we got out of school and—"

"And it's working out for you. You're going off to college. You'll make new friends and make a new life for yourself." Charlie turned his head away and brushed a fist across his eyes. "What do I have? Life as I knew it is over. I'm losing my best friend to college. My mom doesn't want me living with her anymore, so I'm losing the only place I've ever called home. I'm homeless and have no friends. What am I supposed to do with the rest of my miserable life?" Charlie was sniffling, and I wondered if he was crying.

"Charlie, it's not like that. We'll still hang out," I said. "I'll come home every weekend or you can come up to Hammond. It'll be fun."

"And I'll still be around," Brett offered.

"Y'all have no idea what my life was like before high school, before I met Abe." Charlie struggled to get the words out. "I had nowhere to go to be happy. I hated being home, and I hated school. My mom didn't care about me, and everybody at school picked on me. No matter what I did, nobody liked me. You were my only friend."

"That's not true, Charlie. You have lots of friends. You've had lots of girlfriends, too."

Charlie shook his head. "They were your friends. They only tolerated me because of you. Heck, the only reason no one picked on me in high school is because they were afraid of you."

"That's not true."

"High school was the best time of my life. I don't want it to end...ever."

"I loved high school, too," I said slowly. "It was some of the best years of my life, but...but those times are over. We have to move on."

Charlie turned to face me, tears flowing free. "You know why my mom wants me to move out? Huh? Do you?"

I shook my head slowly, shocked Charlie was so emotional. I didn't know what to say or how to act. Brett looked uncomfortable, too, like he wasn't supposed to be hearing the conversation.

"Her new boyfriend wants to move into our house, but he doesn't want to be bothered by a teenage son." Charlie wiped a stream of tears from his face. "So, she's kicking me out of the house, just so she can live with her free-loading boyfriend. She's choosing some loser over her own flesh and blood." Charlie pumped his fist in the air. "My dad would kill that leech if he was still alive!"

"I'm so sorry, Charlie. I had no idea that—"

"You're not too sorry. You're going off to college and leaving me all alone."

I lowered my head. That stung. The only reason Charlie wasn't coming to college with me was because he didn't make a high enough score on his ACT.

"I'm your friend, Charlie." Brett's voice was low and cracked a bit. "And it's not because of Abe. I know how it feels to move to a new place—a place where no one knows you. It's not fun. But you know what? You made it easy for me. You were the first person to become friends with me, and I'll never forget it. I'm not going to college, so I'll be around. You won't be alone."

CHAPTER 8

Charlie set off down the trail, and Brett and I followed. We walked in silence for an hour. The only sound I heard outside of the crunching of our feet and birds chirping was an occasional sniffle from Charlie. That was easily one of the top three worst days of my life. Charlie was my best friend, and I hated seeing him like that. I felt powerless and extremely guilty. Since going back to high school was not an option, I didn't know what to do to make things better for him.

The trail ahead of us veered sharply to the right. According to Charlie's map, it was supposed to run parallel to Betham Creek for another two miles until it intersected with Rocky Creek Trail and the very spot where North Carolina native Jennifer Banks had disappeared.

"Can you hear Betham Creek?" Charlie asked.

Charlie's voice was so sudden and unexpected that I jumped. "Jesus," I said, "you scared me. It didn't even sound like you."

"I'm glad I'm not the only one he scared." Brett shook his head. "It sounded like you saw something bad up ahead."

"Sorry. It's been so long since I said anything that my voice just got away from me a bit. It went off a bit louder than I expected."

Charlie stopped walking at the point where the trail met up with the creek and waited for us to catch up. When we were beside him, he stared down at his feet. "No one needs to know about back there, right?"

"Are you for real?" I asked. "First off, who would we tell? Second, you're the only person to ever see me cry."

"A lot of people have seen me cry." Brett shrugged. "I'm not ashamed."

"I actually believe you." Charlie laughed, and I was happy to see the Charlie I knew so well. "Thanks. Y'all are good friends."

"Abe, you really cried before?"

Charlie held up a finger. "Once, but it didn't count."

"What do you mean, it didn't count?" Brett wanted to know.

"Because it was a happy cry—the night the Saints won the Super Bowl."

I smiled at the memory, wondering if I'd ever see another Saints' championship. Glad to have my friend back, I whistled as we walked. The creek to our left was wider than the one we'd left behind at the picnic area and appeared deeper. The sun sparkled off the water, and an occasional trout flipped into the air and then landed with a splash. Although we had eaten only an hour ago, my stomach was starting to grumble. "Where do y'all want to eat tonight?"

"What about McDonald's?" Charlie asked.

Brett shook his head. "Dude, we're staying in that cabin near Gatlinburg and—thanks to you—we've got lots of money. Let's live it up a little."

"What's there to eat in Gatlinburg?" Charlie asked.

"I saw a Hard Rock Café when we drove through the main strip," I offered. "Want to try it?"

Charlie nodded. "Sounds good. I've never eaten a hard rock, but I'd try anything twice—or three times."

"You don't know what the Hard Rock Café is?" Brett asked.

"He knows what the Hard Rock Café is," I said.

Charlie nodded "Yeah, we ate at one in Memphis when I was a kid. Abe and I ate at the one in New Orleans a couple of times."

We made small talk as we continued on our way. The trail was wider than the others we'd traveled on, but was littered with fallen trees and broken branches, making the hike more difficult and time consuming. What should have taken an hour took at least two, and we breathed a sigh of relief when we saw the sign for the Rocky Creek Trail. We stopped at the fork in the trail and dropped our rucksacks.

"This is it." Charlie pulled out the camera and took more pictures. "This is where Jennifer Banks' boyfriend was supposed to meet her."

I walked to the edge of the creek and dug through my bag until I found the poster for Jennifer. She had gone missing on June 25, 2010, so it was unlikely we would find any evidence of her existence—if she was ever here in the first place. According to her boyfriend—some guy named Ray—they were hiking the backcountry and Jennifer had become tired and refused to take another step. Ray had wanted to hike to the end of Betham Creek Trail, so he told Jennifer to wait for him by the fork in the trail. When he returned a couple of hours later, he claimed she was gone.

"You think Jennifer's boyfriend was telling the truth?" I asked Charlie.

"The cops sure didn't. According to that article, they believed Jennifer had been murdered back at her home and they publicly named Ray as a suspect in her disappearance."

"But you said the cops thought they all committed suicide by tree or something," Brett said.

"That's what the park rangers said, but the detectives in Jennifer's home town said her dad called the cops two different times before she disappeared to report that Ray hit Jennifer." Charlie pulled out his phone to verify the information. "Yeah, that's it. They said he was accused of domestic violence or something, but Jennifer denied it all when the cops talked to her. When she disappeared, her dad said she'd wanted to end the relationship, but was afraid of Ray."

"So..." Brett was thoughtful. "She was never here? He just pretended she was here to cover up her murder?"

Charlie shrugged. "All I know is the cops have no clue what they're talking about and the rangers have no clue what they're doing."

"But you do?" Brett rolled his eyes.

I wanted to mess around in the creek, but I didn't want to get wet again, now that my clothes were dry, so I tucked the poster away and stepped back. "Y'all ready to keep going? If we hurry, we should be able to make these seven miles in three hours, or so, and be at the Hard Rock Café before dark."

Charlie picked up a branch, balancing it in his hand. "I thought there'd be more to see at the spots where they disappeared. You know how they have those crosses on the side of the road to let you know someone died there? I thought there'd be at least that, but there's nothing at all."

I nodded. "If we didn't know about the article and the posters, we'd have no idea what happened here."

Charlie tossed the branch into the creek and turned to leave. "Let's get this done so we can go eat some hard rocks."

We took turns taking the lead along Rocky Creek Trail, which was narrower than any we'd seen to that point. Although it wasn't wide, it seemed well trodden and was easier than expected to navigate. Rocky Creek flowed in the same direction we were walking and zigzagged from one side of the trail to the other. When the creek crossed the trail, we were forced to cross swinging bridges that appeared to be held together by thread. At one such crossing, the wooden bridge hung about fifteen feet above the creek. The trail appeared to dip sharply on the other side of the bridge and return to a level even with that of the creek.

Before long, I glanced at Charlie's map and counted the amount of times the creek crossed the trail. Six. On the fifth crossing, and right before the first of three switchbacks along the trail, was the spot where Woody Lawson went missing—and less than a mile from where Joy was last seen. "How many creek crossings did we pass?" I asked.

Charlie and Brett stopped and turned to me. Charlie scrunched his face, counting in his head. "Four of them."

I located the fourth crossing on the map. "We're almost there."

"Is that where Joy disappeared?" Brett asked.

Charlie shook his head. "Some kid named Woody Lawson from Ohio."

"He was the youngest to disappear," I said. "He was only fifteen."

"Is he the one who wanted to try out for the Olympic swim team?" Brett asked.

Charlie nodded.

Brett frowned. "What happened to him?"

"He'd been hiking right along here with his church group and decided to jog ahead, wanting to take the opportunity to get in some endurance training." Charlie rolled his eyes. "I've always had a problem with people who were so dedicated to working out that they felt the need to do it even when they were on vacation."

I dug Woody's poster out of my bag and went over every detail again. The youth leaders had insisted Woody wait for the rest of the group at the first switchback, so there wouldn't be too much trail distance between them. When the rest of the group reached the switchback an hour later, Woody wasn't there. The youth leaders assumed Woody had gotten tired of waiting for them and had continued up the trail, so they kept the group moving until they reached the Tipton Bluffs Bypass Trail, which led to the Tipton Bluffs parking lot. When they made it to the church van, Woody was not there, and they started to panic. They searched the bathrooms and surrounding area, but when darkness fell they still hadn't found Woody. The date was June 19, 2007, and it was the last day Woody Lawson was ever seen. Although it had been six years, the area where he'd disappeared was the closest to where Joy had disappeared, and it might yield some clues.

I tucked away the poster and map, and we walked on. We knew we were nearing the fifth switchback when the other portion of the trail appeared through the trees to our left. When we reached the bottom of the horseshoe-shaped trail, I stopped and looked around. The surrounding forest was thick with green and brown underbrush, along with spots of orange leaves. "Is this where Woody Lawson went missing?" I asked.

Charlie nodded. "That's what the article claims."

I thought about that for a second. "How do they know that?"

"What do you mean?" Charlie asked.

"This is where the youth pastors and the rest of the church group were supposed to meet him, but he wasn't here," I said.

Charlie shrugged. "Right. So?"

"How do they know he even made it here? What if he went missing a hundred yards that way"—I pointed in the direction from which we had just hiked—"or halfway to the van? Why did they call this spot the disappearance site?"

"Good point, Detective Abraham." Charlie pulled out the camera and took some pictures. "I guess we can't know for sure where any of them went missing—including Joy. All we know is where she was last seen."

"Yeah," I said. "They all could've gone off trail anywhere from where they were last seen to where they were supposed to be and gotten eaten by a bear or something."

"What if they tripped and fell off one of those cliffs back there?" Brett asked. "Or fell off a bridge like the one back there? They could've plunged to the bottom of the mountain and never been seen again."

I nodded. "The first thing the park rangers do is search the trails when someone goes missing and then they start searching off-trail. But if they don't know exactly where they went off the trail, it would be next to impossible to find them."

Charlie sat on a nearby rock. "Aren't y'all tired?"

"No," I said, "but my back aches from when you pushed me on those rocks."

Charlie laughed. "I wish I would've had the camera in my hand to shoot that. It looked like you were moving in slow motion, with your body all twisted like a pretzel. Even your scream came out s-l-o-w-l-y."

"I didn't scream."

"Yes, you did," Brett said. "You screamed like you were being murdered."

"I didn't scream, and I wasn't twisted like a pretzel. I went down gracefully, like a sleek panther pouncing from one rock to the other, stalking its prey. I landed lightly on my back in the guard position, luring my opponent into my trap, where I would've arm-barred him into submission had he even tried to mess with me."

"Yeah, that's not how it looked from where we stood," Charlie said.

I waved him off and stretched my back, wondering what was wrong with it. I had tried to ignore the dull pain as we hiked and was successful in doing so, but now that we'd stopped, it was starting to intensify. I'd broken a bone in my back a few years earlier when I'd jerked the wrong way while grappling one of the linemen from football. I was hoping I hadn't aggravated the injury.

Charlie reached into one of his pockets and pulled out his phone. "Still no service."

"What time is it?" Brett asked.

"Almost four."

I glanced up at the trees, trying to see through the thick green leaves that covered the forest like a heavy canopy. Other than a few tiny slivers of blue, I couldn't see the sky. "It looks more like eight o'clock."

Charlie nodded. "The forest is either getting thicker or the weather's getting bad because it's definitely darker than it was when we turned onto this trail."

Almost as if on cue, thunder rumbled in the distance. "Holy smokes," Brett said, "what if it starts raining?"

"We need to hurry. I want to make it to where Joy disappeared before the rain comes." I scowled. "I unpacked my raingear this morning."

"I did, too." Readjusting his rucksack on his shoulders, Charlie strode down the trail and called over his shoulder, "Last one to the end of the trail is a wet rat."

Brett and I followed Charlie. Our legs pumped like pistons as we made the brisk descent down the steep trail, fueled by the approaching thunder. After fifty yards, Rocky Creek Trail horseshoed again and that switchback set us on our original course and the creek was once again flowing along the trail. It was on our right this time, and there was something about it that gave me pause. I stopped to try to figure it out.

"What is it?" Charlie asked, looking back at me.

I studied the creek for several seconds. "There's something different about it."

Brett readjusted his bag. "Who cares? We need to get out of here before that storm reaches us."

It suddenly occurred to me and I pointed. "Look—the rocks are gone."

Charlie shrugged. "And?"

"That happens in the Ozarks." Brett shook his head. "If we don't get out of here in a hurry, we're going to be swimming."

"I'm not worried," Charlie said. "It's impossible for me to drown."

Brett cocked his head sideways. "I heard someone at school say you could hold your breath forever."

"Not forever—four minutes," I corrected.

"Wow! That's awesome!" Brett said.

"Don't encourage him." I glanced at the clouds gathering overhead. "He could damage his brain holding his breath too long."

Charlie laughed. "That's a myth. My brain will be fine."

"Is it true you pulled a stunt on the girls' swim team freshman year?"

"He stayed under water for over three minutes and pretended he drowned so one of the girls would give him mouth-to-mouth." I laughed. "He came alive right quick when the coach started to put his mouth on him."

Brett stared at Charlie as though he were a super hero. "When'd you first realize you could hold your breath for so long?"

"When I was about three. I used to lie on my face in the bathtub and hum. I didn't think it was a big deal until my mom came in screaming one day. She thought I was dead." Charlie walked to the edge of the creek and studied the rising water, chuckling. "It was great. From that moment on, I loved freaking people out. My record's four minutes. I want to be able to hold it for six by the time I'm twenty.

"You'd better stop," I warned. "It's too dangerous and—"

"Hey!" Charlie said. "Something moved in the trees across the creek."

Brett and I rushed to where he stood and followed his gaze. The trees were thick, the shadows dark.

"Where?" I asked.

"To the right of that giant tree—the one shaped like a V."

The tree had algae or some sort of green stuff growing at the base of it. I detected no movement anywhere near it, other than the swaying of the surrounding underbrush. "I don't see anything."

"Something was there!" Charlie nodded his head in excited certainty. "It walked across the open space behind that V."

"Was it a bear?" Brett asked.

Charlie shook his head. "It was weird. It walked like a person, but it wasn't shaped like a person."

"Big Foot?" I could hear the fear in Brett's voice.

I was surprised Charlie didn't laugh or make fun of Brett.

"Big Foot doesn't exist," I said. "It could've been a tree swaying in the wind. It's hard to make out things in the shadows."

"Let's get out of here," Brett said.

"We've come this far," I said, "and I'm not leaving until I see where Joy disappeared."

"Why don't we come back tomorrow, when whatever Charlie saw is gone?" Brett offered.

"We're close." I pointed in the direction we had to go. "It's just down the trail. Maybe twenty minutes. We need to get there before it starts raining and washes more evidence away."

"But what about the river? The water's come up about three feet already." Brett looked up to the tops of the mountains. "It must be storming something fierce up there."

"Abe's right," Charlie said. "It could've been a tree swaying."

I knew instantly Charlie was only trying to make Brett feel better. I tried to penetrate the shadows, wondering what he saw.

"The rain is coming fast," Brett said. "We need to turn around before we get caught in it."

"We won't be able to make it back to the truck before the rain hits anyway," Charlie said. "Let's go see where Joy disappeared and then get to higher ground."

I turned from the river to look at Brett. "You in?"

He sighed. "Yeah, I'm with you guys, but let's hurry so we can get away from the river bank. It's dangerous during a storm."

Propelled by a sense of urgency and fear, we hiked as though we were in a power-walking marathon. No matter how fast we walked, we couldn't get ahead of the rumbling thunder barreling down on us. The forest grew darker, and it became difficult to see more than a dozen feet ahead of us. The wind became stronger. The trees rocked back and forth. They groaned and squeaked as they rubbed against each other. Leaves broke free from the branches above and, after being tossed violently about, rained down onto the forest floor. I could smell the rain coming.

"Abe, you need to check your map." Charlie had to raise his

voice so he could be heard over the wind and thunder. "There's a split in the trail. That's got to be where Rocky Creek meets up with Rocky Ridge."

I hurried forward, reaching for the map as I walked. "That can't be."

"We passed it?" Brett asked.

I stretched out the map. The cool wind whipped it around and I had to fold it tight in order to steady it. I looked to my right and couldn't see the river. According to what Mr. Vincent had said, Joy disappeared along Rocky Creek Trail where the river ended in a seventy-foot waterfall. If I was reading the map right, we'd overshot the waterfall by a mile. "Are we sure this is the end of Rocky Creek? I never noticed the waterfall."

"It would've been hard to hear because of the thunder and wind," Charlie reasoned.

Brett pointed to a rugged sign almost hidden by waist-high weeds. "Yep—that way is Rocky Ridge Trail and that way is Tipton Bluffs Bypass."

Charlie consulted the news article on his phone. "This is where Katherine Turner disappeared. We passed Joy's spot."

I remembered Katherine Turner. She'd stuck out because she was also from Louisiana. She and her high school sweetheart had eloped and gotten married at one of the roadside chapels in Gatlinburg. They were exploring the area of the Tipton Bluffs Bypass Trail when they were separated for a brief moment. Her new husband said he turned around and Katherine was gone—there one second and gone the next. "We need to go back."

Brett stared longingly down Tipton Bluff's Bypass Trail. "I think we should try to get to Tipton's Bluff through here. According to the map, it's only two miles from here to the truck. Even if it is rough, I think it would be better than going all the way back."

I shook my head. "It's not rough—it's impassable. A tornado tore through here last summer and they haven't been able to clear it out yet."

"But what if they did and you just don't know about it?" Brett asked.

"We could check." I tucked the map back in my pocket. Thunder roared overhead and a brilliant flash of lightning startled all of us. "Let's go back. We need to keep our eyes out for the waterfall."

Charlie glanced up at the umbrella of trees overhead. They swayed fiercely to and fro. "Maybe we should start looking for shelter."

"Whatever we do," Brett said, "I have to go—and I don't mean pee."

"You can't wait?" I asked.

"Nope—it's that time of the day for me. My stomach is killing me. I won't be able to make it back if I don't go now, and I want to go while it's still dry out here."

"I'm cool with it." Charlie pulled off his rucksack. "My neck is killing me. I need a break."

"Try to hurry. That storm sounds like it's bearing down on us." I tore off my rucksack, too, and took a seat on a nearby log. The wind had gotten markedly cooler and pierced my wet back. I shuddered, watching as Brett picked his way off the trail to find a spot to use it. "Don't go too far."

"I'm just going behind that clump of bushes." The wind and thunder muffled Brett's voice, but I made out his words.

CHAPTER 9

I found myself worrying about Joy. Earlier, I'd been satisfied she was hiding out with her aunt, but now I started getting that panicky feeling in my gut again. What if she really wasn't with her aunt? What if I walked away and left her out here in the wilderness somewhere—fighting for her life, just waiting for someone to come along and save her? I remembered the night of our first date, and my eyes filled with tears. I turned and nonchalantly wiped my eyes with my shoulders, trying to dismiss the memory. She was such a good person. Honest and loyal. I scowled. "Why did I break up with her again?"

I caught movement out of the corner of my eye and turned to see Charlie roll off a log and to a seated position on the ground. "You said something?"

"Talking to myself." I looked toward the spot where I'd last seen Brett. "How long does he need to take a crap?"

"I can usually read a whole comic book on the toilet." Charlie grunted. "It's the only place I get peace from my mom."

I heard a tapping sound to my right and turned to look. I couldn't detect the source of the noise. There was another, then another. They increased in number and speed. Suddenly, a marble-sized droplet of rain landed on the bridge of my nose and splashed across my cheeks and I realized what was happening. "Hurry, Brett! The rain is here!"

More droplets broke through the umbrella of leaves and began pelting us like bullets from a machine gun. Thunder clapped and lightning flashed. I jerked. Charlie and I jumped to our feet and shrugged into our rucksacks.

Charlie took a step in the direction of the clump of trees and hollered for Brett. There was no response. Charlie turned to me, his eyes wide. I rushed passed him and rounded the edge of the bushes. My heart fell to my water shoes.

"Brett! Brett!" I stared wildly about. Charlie rushed up, and I shook my head. "He's not here."

Charlie pushed and pulled at the bushes surrounding the tiny clearing. "Brett, this isn't funny!"

The rain began to fall harder and faster, and my hair and clothes were soon completely saturated. Cold water flowed down my neck and splashed over my body. I shivered, as I scanned the area. Visibility was low. All I could see through the gray sheets of rain were the dim outlines of the surrounding trees and Charlie standing directly beside me. I trembled, and I didn't know if it was from fear or the cold.

"Brett! Where are you?"

"This can't be happening," Charlie screamed. He turned to me. "What do we do?"

The pelting rain brutalized the ground and made it impossible for our untrained eyes to see a track. I quickly calculated the time in my head. It couldn't have been more than five minutes since he disappeared around the corner of the bushes. In that terrain, he couldn't have gone far. "Fan out. You go that way, and I'll go this way."

Charlie shook his head. "I'm not leaving your side."

Instead of arguing, I ran to my right and plunged into the thicket, scanning the area as I ran, trying to take in as much as I could. I could feel Charlie on my heels. Branches whipped at my face and tore at my arms. Rain attacked from above. "Brett! Where are you?"

We reached what looked like a game trail, and Charlie grabbed me by the back of my shirt and pulled hard. I turned. He pointed off in the distance, but didn't speak—he couldn't speak. He began to back up slowly. I looked where he pointed and gasped. A large creature was moving through the trees in the distance, and it had Brett's limp body slung over its shoulder. Bile instantly rushed up to my throat, choking me. I spat the bitter liquid to the side and pulled out Jezebel. Gripping it firmly in my hand, I raced toward Brett's location, screaming as I ran.

The creature must have heard me above the noise of the storm because it turned and looked in my direction. I couldn't discern a color or shape—couldn't even tell if it had a face—but it moved like a human. It looked like its skin was made of leaves. When it stopped moving, it blended perfectly with the background, as though it were a part of the forest. All I could make out was Brett dangling. He looked like he was suspended in mid-air.

In one quick motion, Leaf Creature dipped its frame to one side, and Brett collapsed in a heap to the ground—he didn't move. Fear choked me as I rushed forward and reduced the seventy-yard gap between us. I lifted Jezebel in front of me and continued to scream as loud as I could, hoping it would intimidate Leaf Creature. It suddenly lifted an arm and pointed it in my direction. A brilliant flash of orange light shot from its limb. Dirt kicked up in front and to the left of me just as the sound of an explosion reached my ears. Before I could take another step, I was knocked sprawling.

"It's got a gun!" It was Charlie, and he was on top of me. "We need to get out of here!"

We scrambled to our feet. Leaf Creature was running now—directly toward us. Another shot rang out and bark from a nearby tree sprayed into my face, stinging my flesh. I turned, and Charlie was already gone. I raced toward the trail and caught sight of Charlie's backside breaking a path through the trees. The trail was indiscernible. There was another explosion behind me—that one sounded closer.

Charlie was yelling. Although I could barely hear him above the barrage of thunder and the pounding rain, it was enough to guide my way. Lightning flashed nearby, and there was a thunderous crack followed by what sounded like a repetition of shotgun blasts. I jumped in my skin. Did Leaf Creature have reinforcements? I caught a flash of movement through the rain directly in front of me and realized the source of the blasting noise. My heart was paralyzed for a split second, as I processed what I was seeing.

Before I could react, Charlie appeared out of nowhere and slammed a shoulder into my chest, directing me away from the falling tree. We both slammed into the ground just as the giant tree crashed to the forest floor several yards away from us. The earth shuddered from the tremendous impact. Twigs and other debris rained down on us. I scrambled to my feet and glanced behind us. I didn't see anything.

Charlie was already up. "Come on! We need to get out of here."

I hesitated. "What about Brett?"

"You saw him—he's dead. But we're alive, and we need to get out of here before that thing comes here and kills us, too."

Flashes of brilliance lit up the area, and I caught a glimpse of the trail. I pointed. "That way! Run!"

Charlie and I fled down the trail, heading back toward the

switchback where Woody Lawson had gone missing. Charlie was leading the way. As we ran and the rain fell harder, I lost sight of him through the sheets of water. I had to brush water from my eyes constantly so I could make sure I was headed along the trail. I caught a glimpse of Charlie when the lightning flashed again, and I continued straight ahead, wondering how he could see the trail. I heard more crashing sounds as the roots of other trees lost their battle with the wind and collapsed to the ground all around us. I felt like we were in a minefield.

I turned several times to look over my shoulder, but I didn't see Leaf Creature again. *Maybe one of the trees smashed him!* I began to think it might be safe to go back and check on Brett, but fear kept me going down the trail. Lightning flashed again and a wave of panic washed over me as I realized Charlie was gone. One second he was there, and the next second he was gone. Had Leaf Creature circled around and snatched Charlie right out from in front of me? Was he using the storm as cover to take us out one at a time?

I started to slow down. Lightning flashed again and I saw nothing—just dark and utter emptiness. The ground had disappeared from under my feet. There was a brief moment when I felt suspended in the air, as though everything had frozen in place, but it was extremely short-lived. I shot straight downward. My stomach tickled. It felt like my heart had lifted to my throat. Tree branches blurred by and some of them slapped me as I plunged toward the earth.

Almost as suddenly as I'd begun falling, my freefall came to an abrupt halt in a body of deep and icy water. I hadn't prepared for the sudden rush of water that got sucked into my mouth and up my nose. The current immediately took control of my body and dragged me downriver. I kicked my feet and swung my arms in a desperate attempt to slow my rapid descent to the bottom of the angry river. My lungs ached. I choked on the water that had slipped down my throat. I resisted the burning desire to take a breath, as I fought to get back to the surface. I kicked in desperation and paddled with my hands. My arms and legs burned. My lungs felt like they were about to explode. I didn't think I was going to make it.

At long last, I reached the surface of the water and sucked in a lungful of air. I coughed, water spraying from my throat. I felt myself being driven downriver by the powerful current. Rocks zipped by and I crashed into some of them, altering my course. I was like a human pinball, bouncing from rock to rock, trying desperately to keep my head above water and to get off the violent rollercoaster ride.

I didn't know how far down the river I'd shot and I didn't know what river I'd fallen into, but it didn't look like any creek we had encountered on our hike. Although it was considerably brighter along the river than it had been in the thick of the forest, I couldn't make out the surrounding landscape through the driving rain. I thought I caught a fleeting glimpse of a large shadowy figure way up on the riverbank, but I couldn't be sure. Was it Leaf Creature? Did he have Charlie?

I tried to clutch onto passing rocks, but my hands slipped on the green slime that covered the smooth surfaces. Just when I thought I couldn't stay afloat any longer, my legs and arms began to drag the bottom of the river. I tried to stand, but the rushing force knocked me over and I plunged face first into the water, breathing in as I went under. I came up gasping for air and tried to right myself. I used my hands and feet to push off the bottom and steered myself toward the nearest riverbank.

After a long and exhausting struggle, I managed to reach shallow water and crawled toward a large rock that stood like a centurion at the edge of the river. My rucksack serving as a cushion, I leaned against the rock. I was battered and exhausted, my arms aching from the intense workout. I shivered as I tried to catch my breath and get my bearings. The pelting rain had been reduced to a steady dribble, and the clouds were starting to dissipate, allowing me to make out my surroundings. I was in a wide river surrounded by steep cliffs. I reached for the map in my pocket and it was only then that I realized I still clutched Jezebel in a death grip.

I scanned the area. Everything looked clear. I holstered Jezebel and pulled out a mushy mess that used to be a map. I tried to unfold it, but the paper was stuck together and began to tear as I forced the folds apart. I silently cursed myself for destroying the only two maps we had. I'd have to rely on my memory, but that would do no good because I didn't remember seeing a major river running through this area. Other than Rocky Creek and Betham Creek, there were three fingers of creeks that extended northward, but they looked much smaller than this on the map.

I stood on shaky legs, steadying myself with a hand on the large rock, and winced when the pain in my back reverberated through my body. I had to find Charlie. Had he fallen into the river, too? Or had he detected the cliff before we reached it and avoided it? What if Leaf Creature got to him? What if he'd been killed as well? My jaw burned with emotion. I shook my head to clear my thoughts, then made my way along the rock and climbed up onto the riverbank.

Smaller pebbles littered the soft ground and made walking easier. I trudged around the large rock and began following the river, calling for Charlie as I walked. My voice boomeranged back to me. I scanned the surrounding cliffs, searching for a way up the vertical walls of rock. There was none.

"Charlie!" I called again and again, keeping a wary eye out for Leaf Creature. I trembled. My mind was numb. *How is this happening to us? This can't be real!*

Up ahead was another large rock that stood about ten feet high. It was either go over it or get back into the river to get around it. Still shivering, I reached for a handhold and pulled myself up. Utilizing a toehold here and a handhold there, I picked my way up the face of the rock. When I reached the top, I stood and took advantage of my elevated position. The rain had stopped now, and the sun was shining again. I welcomed the warmth.

"Charlie," I screamed and paused as my voice echoed down the river. I was about to yell again when I realized the last echo was not my voice. I stood on my tiptoes and shaded my eyes. "Charlie?"

"Abe!"

Shielding the sun from my eyes with both hands, I scanned the area. I looked upriver from where I had come and then downriver. That was when I saw him. He was a hundred yards downriver, on the opposite riverbank, and he was jumping up and down waving his arms in the air. His shirt and shorts clung to his body and his wet hair was plastered to his pale scalp. He looked like one of those wet muskrats I used to trap back in Louisiana when I was a kid.

"I'm coming!" Almost crying with relief, I made my way down the opposite side of the rock, half climbing and half falling.

When I was still a couple of feet from the ground, my rucksack snagged on a rock that jutted out from the boulder, and I was left hanging, my feet dangling. I kicked and jerked like a baby hanging from a bouncer. The strap finally broke free and I fell in a heap. I jumped to my feet and jogged along the riverbank toward where I had last seen Charlie. The going was tough. I had to jump over a large rock here and dodge a fallen tree branch there, but I finally reached a point along the river where I could see Charlie again. I was surprised to see he was already in the water, struggling to reach my side of the river. He would take two steps toward my side of the river, then get knocked over, and tumble several yards down river. I kept moving, trying to stay parallel with him.

"Be careful," I said. "If your foot gets stuck under a rock, you'll drown."

Charlie stopped to take a breath, holding onto a jagged rocked. "I don't think I have the strength to make it."

He was twenty feet away. I shrugged off my rucksack and searched inside for the rope I had packed. I grabbed it and quickly searched my surroundings for a stout branch. When I found one, I tied an end of the rope to the branch and wrapped the other end around my arm. "You ready, Charlie?"

Charlie nodded, stretching out a hand. I reached back with the branch and tossed it as hard as I could. It landed with a splash directly in front of him and rushed toward him. Releasing his hold on the rock, he clutched at the branch and pulled it close to his chest. Hooking one arm around a tree, I held onto the rope with my other arm and groaned when it went taut and bit into my flesh. I stood like an anchor, while Charlie pulled himself toward me, hand over hand. When he reached the river's edge, I hauled him from the water. He collapsed to the ground and rolled onto his back. I dropped beside him and stretched, using my rucksack as a pillow.

"I thought you'd drowned."

"You know I can hold my breath forever," Charlie said between gasps. "I have to admit, though, that current is strong."

"Yeah. I thought I'd reached the end of the line." I propped up on an elbow, facing Charlie. "What happened back there? Did you even see the drop off?"

Charlie's eyes were closed, and his face was turned toward the sun. "One minute I was running along that trail, and the next minute I was skydiving without a parachute."

"Where did this river come from? It's not on the map."

Keeping his eyes closed, Charlie shook his head. "I don't even know."

Ignoring the pain in my back, I stood slowly. I studied the wall behind us and searched for a way up. "We need to climb up there so we can get our bearings."

"I just want to sleep," Charlie said.

"We don't have time to sleep. We need to get out of here before it gets dark. If we get trapped out here overnight with Leaf Creature, we're as good as dead."

"Abe, I really think that was some kind of mountain monster. It didn't look human, and it didn't look like an animal."

"I think you're right." I continued searching for a way up, but there was no scaling the wall where we were. I returned the rope to my rucksack and shouldered it, then began moving downriver. "With or without you, Charlie."

Charlie groaned loudly. "Just let me die in peace."

"Nobody's dying just yet, but if you stay here alone, you will." I didn't look back. There was a sharp bend in the river up ahead, and I wanted to see what was beyond it. Somewhere along the way Charlie caught up to me and we rounded the bend together. It looked like the rock wall was tapering downward in the distance.

"It looks lower over there," Charlie said. Something fell in the woods behind us and Charlie spun around. "Did you hear that?"

I nodded, then tried to penetrate the trees with my eyes. "We need to keep going."

We walked until the rock wall all but disappeared and allowed us access to the forest to the right. We plunged into the trees and made the gradual ascent to the top of the cliff and walked along its edge, hoping to make it back to the spot where we'd fallen before night fell. I didn't relish returning to that area because of Leaf Creature, but we had to get to that trail if we wanted to get back to the truck and call for help. Without a map, we could very well end up like the others who went missing. I dismissed the thought, told myself everything would be fine, and labored on.

Tall trees grew along the cliff's edge, and I began to shiver again in the cool shade. "I don't think I've ever been this cold in the summertime before."

"I know. I can't stop my teeth from chattering."

There were no discernible trails that we could see, so we had to force our way through the thick underbrush. We arrived at an ocean of thick briar patches that extended in front of us for what seemed like forever, smothering the bases of the many trees that sprang up from its midst. I tried to push my way through it, but for my efforts, only managed to get stabbed in the legs and thighs by dozens of needle-sharp thorns.

"There's no way we can make it through this crap," Charlie said.

I looked up at the forest ceiling. There was no mistaking the fact the sun was going down. If we had to go around the thorns it would take us miles out of our way. I walked to the edge of the cliff and looked down. It was clearly twenty or more feet to the ground level of the riverbank. "I guess we have to go around."

Without wasting any more time, we stabbed our way through the trees to the left and sank deeper and deeper into the Blue Summit Mountains National Forest. As we struggled through the underbrush, we encountered more briar patches and had to deviate from our course of travel a dozen or so times. We tried to keep track of our location as we made our way through the maze of briar patches and attempted to head back toward the river, but it seemed impossible. Each time I thought we were close to getting back the edge of the cliff that overlooked the river, we encountered more thorny bushes and had to turn away. It was dizzying, and I soon realized we had gotten so turned around that we didn't know which way was up. I stopped near a giant tree and dropped to the ground in despair. Darkness was falling, and we were lost.

"We're not going to make it out of here tonight," I said.

"I kind of had that one figured." Charlie stared around us. "Mother Nature's got us wrapped tight in her razor wire and she won't let us go."

I stared upward, but it was no use. "I can't even see the sun to try and figure out which way is west."

"Even if you could," Charlie said, "we don't know where we are, so we won't know which way to head to get out of this hellhole."

I leaned forward, slid my rucksack off my shoulders and took in our immediate surroundings. Walls of dense briar patches strangled the giant dogwood trees that grew like proud centurions all around us. The trees appeared to have been growing for hundreds of years and looked tall enough to reach the heavens. I wondered if ours were the first human eyes to behold this section of the Blue Summit Mountains. I posed this question to Charlie.

"It doesn't look like anyone has ever been here," he said. "I think this is one of those virgin forests I've read about that's never seen a human footprint."

"It's so weird not to see any trails. It's like we're the only people on the face of the earth." I stood and walked around this natural clearing that would have to serve as our home for the night. "As much as I hate to admit it, I think we're stuck here until tomorrow morning. We'll need to gather up some firewood and prepare a camp before it gets too dark."

"How're we supposed to make a fire?" Charlie asked.

"Crap! I left the matches." My stomach sank. I'd forgotten that small detail. Fire was necessary to keep us safe from bears and any other wild animals that might be lurking around. "If we plan to survive the night, we're going to have to make a fire."

Charlie's face turned a shade whiter. "Wait—what do you mean by *survive?*"

"We have to worry about more than Leaf Creature. This place is crawling with wild animals that can kill us within seconds. Without fire, we're defenseless. We'll never see them coming. We could die."

Charlie gulped, stared wide-eyed. "How do we make fire?"

"When I was a kid, I read that you can do it by rubbing two sticks together."

Charlie nodded. "Yeah, I saw it in a movie. Let's get it done."

We scrambled around and gathered up leaves and tiny twigs and made a small pile at the center of the clearing. "These are all wet," Charlie said. "There's no way they'll catch fire."

I grabbed two stout twigs and peeled away the wet bark and tested the bare wood underneath. Saturated. I began rubbing them together vigorously, hoping the friction would dry them enough to start the fire. I rubbed for probably three minutes, but it felt like fifteen. The muscles in my hands and arms burned. I stopped rubbing and touched one of the sticks to my cheek. It was barely warm.

"Is it working?" Charlie asked.

"Not at all."

"What're we supposed to do? How're we going to make a fire?"

"I don't know, Charlie. I guess we'll have to try and make do without it." A thought occurred to me. "Maybe it's a good thing that we don't have fire. If we build a fire, Leaf Creature would see us from a mile away."

"That's true." Charlie paced back and forth in the little clearing. "Okay, so we should be safe from the creature because he can't see us, but what do we do if we're attacked by a bear?"

I reached into my pocket for my bear spray and yelped. "My bear spray's gone!"

Charlie frowned. "I lost mine when Leaf Creature was after us. I pulled it out and was going to spray him if he got close, but I dropped it somewhere on the trail."

My heart started to race. That can of bear spray had been a constant source of comfort as we traversed this backcountry, but I now felt naked and vulnerable. "This is it, Charlie. We're doomed."

CHAPTER 10

Within minutes, it was dark. We heard strange sounds from the surrounding forest and an occasional twig snapped in the distance. I'd been in the swamps many, many times at night, but I'd always had a flashlight and a rifle. Charlie and I had even spent the night in the swamps at least a dozen times, but we'd slept up in this ancient oak tree to keep from being eaten by alligators. Even if we could climb these giant trees, we might be safe from Leaf Creature, but we wouldn't be safe from the black bears. Out here, there was no place to hide. We were on our own. My hands shook a bit as I pulled the rope from my rucksack. If I could tie this rope across the one opening in the briar patches, at least it might alert us if an animal or Leaf Creature tried to invade our space.

"Charlie, bring your phone over here," I said. "I need some light."

I couldn't see Charlie. I only knew where he was from the rustling noise he made as he moved toward me. I heard him grunt and knew something was wrong.

"What is it?" I asked.

"My phone's dead. It drowned in the river."

I pulled my phone from my pocket and fumbled with the buttons on it. Nothing lit up. I held it up in front of my face and couldn't even see it. "Leaf Creature could be sitting in my lap and I wouldn't be able to see it."

"This is scary," Charlie said. "I'm really regretting our decision to come here. I mean, what are we supposed to tell Brett's mom?"

"Let's try not to think about that." I reached out in the dark and my hand brushed against soft clothing.

Charlie jumped. "What was that?"

"It was me," I said. "I'm trying to feel the tree that was here earlier."

I heard Charlie stirring beside me. I then felt his hand grab my arm and guide it toward the rough bark. "Here it is."

"Let's put our backs against the tree for protection." I scooted over until my back was pressed against the tree, and I could feel Charlie sitting beside me with his back against the tree. I reached to my belt and pulled Jezebel from her sheath. "You still have the punch knife I gave you?"

"Yeah."

"Get it in your hand and stand ready," I said.

"It's already there, but it would be useless against a gun."

My brows furrowed. "It had to be human."

"What? That creature that killed Brett?"

"Yeah. Animals can't shoot guns."

Charlie grunted. "That makes me feel so much better—"

Twigs snapped nearby. It seemed like a mere dozen feet away. I turned to look in the direction of the noise and then realized how futile it was.

"What was that?" Charlie asked, his voice a whisper.

"I'm not sure." Jezebel felt like an extension of my hand. I clutched it with every ounce of strength in my arm. "It can't be Leaf Creature. There's no way it could've found us by now. We went too far downriver."

"I sure hope you're right."

More twigs snapped. "You think a bear can break through all those briar bushes?"

"How should I know?" Charlie's voice shook.

I tried to slow my heart rate by using the deep breathing exercises I'd used when boxing—inhaling through the nose to a slow count of five, holding for five seconds, exhaling through the mouth to a slow count of five, holding five more seconds, and then repeating. It had always worked wonders in the ring and enabled me to recover faster than my opponents between rounds. It used to always give me great confidence when I would come out at the bell for the next round breathing normally, while my opponent panted like a police canine who had tracked clear across the swamps.

But the breathing exercises weren't working now. My heart pounded so hard in my chest I could hear it in my ears. My breath came in labored gasps. I wasn't ready to die. I had too many plans, too much to do.

A distant howl somewhere to my left caused my heart to skip a beat. I felt Charlie jerk beside me.

"That sounded like a wolf," I said.

Another howl came from somewhere behind us. "You think they know we're here?" Charlie asked.

"They shouldn't be able to get through all those briars. I mean, we're bigger and stronger than wolves and we can't push our way through it."

"But they're lower to the ground," Charlie said. "They might be able to slide under the radar." I heard Charlie move and when he spoke again his voice was up above me. "I think we need to leave this area. We're like turtles sitting on a log. We're completely defenseless."

"No, Charlie, it's safer to stay here. We can't see a thing."

Charlie's shoes crunched against the dry leaves as he walked away from the tree.

"Charlie, get back—"

"Ouch!"

I heard briars rustling and Charlie groaning. I scrambled to my hands and knees and crawled toward the sound, using my hands like antennas to feel my way forward. "Are you okay, Charlie?"

"I tripped."

I crawled into him. "Are you hurt?"

"I've got some spears stuck in me." Charlie groaned with each thorn he pulled out of his skin. I wanted to help, but I couldn't see him. I could tell by his breathing he was scared, and I knew it was up to me to be strong and keep him calm.

"Look…we'll be fine tonight. People camp in this backcountry all the time and they don't get eaten by anything. We'll stay here until daylight and then find our way back to the trail."

"What if we can't find the trail?"

I didn't have an answer for him, so I simply said, "We will."

"And what if Leaf Creature gets us like it got Brett and probably Joy?"

That thought of that creature putting his hands on Joy made my stomach turn. "He won't."

When Charlie had removed the last of the thorns from his body, we felt our way back to the tree and resumed our positions. Every now and then I heard a low grumbling sound and I didn't know if it was Charlie's stomach or mine. "You hungry?" I asked.

"Starving."

"Do you want to eat something now?"

"I'd rather wait until morning. If our food attracts bears, I'd at least like to see them coming."

"Good idea." I leaned the back of my head against the tree and allowed my tired eyes to slide shut. The nightly sounds coaxed me into a false sense of security and I could feel myself slipping into a much-needed slumber.

*   *   *

When I first heard the steady crunching sound, I thought I was lying in my backyard listening to Achilles—my giant German shepherd—eating his dog food. I would often feed him after my workouts and then lie on the ground to recuperate while he ate. The cool breeze blew against my cheeks, and I knew it had to be fall, which meant boxing tournaments would be in full swing soon. The crunching stopped briefly and then a twig snapped. I stirred in my sleep, turning to my side. The ground was uncomfortable, but the soothing sound of Achilles eating his food began again, and I settled into my sleeping position. After a few seconds, another branch snapped and I wondered what could be making that sound in Achilles' dog pen.

I suddenly bolted upright as it all came back to me—Brett being taken by Leaf Creature, the storm, the raging river, the briar patches, and us being lost. I scanned the area and when I saw the bear I started to scream, but it got stuck in my throat. The bear had stopped what he was doing and now stood staring at me with brown beady eyes. He was so close I could smell him. With the exception of his tan eyebrows and snout, his fur was black as the night we had just survived. A dark reddish liquid dripped from his snout and I wondered if it was blood.

I realized my hands were empty and slowly felt around for Jezebel. When I found her, I gripped the handle and lifted it in front of me, pointing one of the blades at the bear. As though trying to smell my intentions, the bear tested the air with his black nose. He then reared up on his hind legs and made the most horrific noise I'd ever heard. My heart pounded in my chest so hard it hurt. The bear stood staring down at me, trying to decide what to do next.

"What's going on?" Charlie stirred beside me and sat up to wipe his face. When his eyes focused on the bear standing over us, he lurched to his feet and made a dash for the opening in the briar patches behind us, screaming as he ran.

This seemed to startle the bear, as it dropped to all fours, turned, and loped off in the opposite direction. I sank against the tree and sighed, nearly peeing my pants. "Charlie," I called halfheartedly.

"It's gone."

I stood on trembling legs and grabbed my rucksack. I pulled it onto my shoulders, snatched up Charlie's bag, and set off in the direction Charlie had disappeared. Whatever energy I'd regained from a good night's sleep had been zapped by the fear of the bear encounter. I wanted to roll up in a little ball and go back to sleep, but, instead, I trudged on, calling for Charlie as I hiked. He wouldn't answer, and I began to fear the worst. At that moment, I felt as alone as I'd ever felt. I swallowed hard, as I tried to imagine what fate had befallen Joy. Had she truly been killed by Leaf Creature? Was she still stumbling around the mountains all alone? Or was she hiding out with her aunt?

I didn't know how far I walked—calling Charlie's name every few steps—but it had to have been twenty minutes before I heard a response to my hollering.

"Over here, Abe."

I stopped and looked in the direction of Charlie's voice. Solid briar patches. "Where are you?"

"Over here," he said.

I searched for a way around the prickly bushes and detected a small passageway through the thinner portion of the thickets. I shucked off my rucksack and, holding it in one hand and Charlie's in the other, I inched sideways through the narrow lane. As I zigzagged along the passageway, I noticed globs of mushy fruit on the ground that were the same color as the dark reddish liquid I'd seen on the bear's snout. My blood ran cold. This trail had been made by a bear. What if we encountered it?

"Charlie, where are you?"

"Here," Charlie said. "I can see you."

I quickly traveled the last stretch of the passageway and finally broke out into a shaded clearing. Charlie had moved away from the briar patches and was standing several yards away at the edge of a rocky river.

"Where are we?" I asked.

"Not sure, but it's a lot nicer than the place we stayed last night."

I threw Charlie's rucksack in his direction. "If you ever leave me to carry your rucksack again, everything in it is mine."

"Knock yourself out. There's nothing in it except the camera, a bottle of water, and a bag of beef jerky."

My thoughts quickly went to food and I remembered how hungry I was. We would need to keep our energy levels up if we planned to survive out there. I sat on a rock near the river and opened my rucksack. Two cans of peaches, a bag of beef jerky, and one bottle of water. "I guess it'll be beef jerky and water for breakfast."

"Breakfast of champions." Charlie pulled his beef jerky out of his bag, and we ate in silence, each of us lost in his own thoughts.

Mine were on Joy and Brett and the hopelessness of our plight. It was all very surreal. We were almost out of food and completely lost. Our best bet was to follow this river and hope it would lead us to civilization. If it didn't, we were in a world of hurt. Sooner or later, Leaf Creature would find us. I turned to Charlie. "Maybe we should preserve some of our water."

"There's a lot of fresh cold water right there." Charlie pointed to the rushing river. "We'll never run out."

"We can't drink that water. What if it's got bacteria in it?"

"We can boil it before we drink— Oh, we don't have any matches."

"No matter. We'll be out of here soon enough. We'll just follow this river until we hit a trail and then follow it to civilization."

Charlie stood and walked to the river, chewing on a mouthful of beef jerky. "Which way do we go?"

I joined him and studied the river to the left first and then to the right. I didn't know what I thought I would see to help me decide which way to go, but, except for the flow of the water, everything looked the same—rocks, rushing water, and dense forestland.

"Well, Captain? Which way do we go?"

I shook my head. "Since we don't know where we are, it's hard to tell."

"If we go the wrong way, we could end up even deeper in the mountains and we'd be at Leaf Creature's mercy."

"I know…so what do we do?"

Charlie chewed on his lower lip for several seconds and then his eyes lit up. "I'll throw my water bottle in the air. When it lands, we'll go in whatever direction the cap is facing."

"Okay," I said. "Do it."

Charlie threw his bottle high into the air. It hit a low-lying branch and ricocheted off it, landing in the river with the cap facing the opposite shore.

"That wasn't an option," I said.

The bottle rocked gently in the water and began floating downriver. Charlie splashed after it and snatched it from the water. He jogged back toward me, high-stepping through the cold water. "I'll do it again."

"Why don't we just follow the flow of the river? It has to lead somewhere."

"Sounds good to me. That way, if we end up lost forever and die out here, it'll be on your conscience, not mine and my bottle."

This river had to lead somewhere important. It looked a lot like the river we had fallen into yesterday afternoon—except it wasn't surrounded by massive cliffs—with its sections of violent whitewater rapids followed by long stretches of calm pools that looked cold and deep. It had the appearance of a sport river, and I almost expected to see a convoy of whitewater rafts and kayaks round the bend to our right.

After we finished eating our beef jerky, we tucked the empty bags away and shouldered our rucksacks.

"Here goes nothing," I said, as we headed off down the riverbank.

CHAPTER 11

Although the sky was bright blue and clear, the area along the riverbank was shady and cool, which kept our sweating to a minimum. Tiny pebbles and smooth rocks lined the shores of the river and we were able to make good time. We said little as we walked. With each mile we hiked, I became more and more concerned we were heading deeper into the backcountry. When I had paced off ten miles, I stopped and turned to Charlie. "Want to take a break?"

He shrugged and stripped off his rucksack. He seemed gloomy. "I guess so."

I dropped my rucksack and walked to the river so I could splash water on my face. As I knelt down on the wet sand at the river's edge, I jumped back when a small trout darted out from under a rock and stabbed at the surface of the water a few feet in front of me. The water was crystal clear and I was able to watch the trout flash back and forth in the pool, feeding on tiny insects walking on the water. I eased my hand into the water and remained motionless until the trout made its way back toward me. When it got within inches of my hand, I raised my arm quickly and was able to hit it with the tips of my fingers, flipping it into the air. It splashed back into the water several feet away and disappeared in the deeper water.

"Hey, Charlie," I said, "how about some fried fish for lunch?"

"That's not even funny."

I splashed the freezing water on my face and sucked air when it hit my chest. After wiping the water from my eyes, I stood and turned to Charlie. He was lying on his back, a forearm covering his face.

"What's wrong, dude?" I asked.

Charlie jerked his arm away from his face and sat up. "What do you mean, *What's wrong?* Brett's dead! We're lost! And I don't mean the kind of lost where you can't find your car in the grocery store parking lot—I mean the kind of lost where you *die!* We don't have any food, we don't have fire—we don't have anything to help us survive this hellhole! Oh, and let's not forget the giant leaf devil thing that's trying to kill us. Great idea coming out here to look for your idiot ex-girlfriend who went and got herself lost or taken or whatever happened to her. Now we're the idiots who are going to die along with her."

I felt my blood starting to rise, but I took a moment to consider where he was coming from. I finally said, in a calm voice, "I understand we're lost, but we have to stay positive. If we lose our cool and panic, there's a good chance we won't survive. My dad always said no matter how bad you're losing a fight, always act like you're winning."

"This is not a boxing match where you win a trophy. Out here, you die!"

"We're not going to die."

"How do you know? None of us thought Brett would die when we came out here, but he did! You can't tell me we won't die. You don't know what'll happen to us."

I nodded, trying to choose my words carefully. I needed Charlie to remain calm, even if it meant lying to him. "I'm sure there's a search party out there right now looking for us and it's only a matter of time before they find us. Don't forget…the park rangers have an excellent record of finding missing people."

"Excellent record? Ask Joy and those other kids about their *excellent* record. I'm betting they don't share your love for the rangers. We're going to end up like them—lost forever and no one will ever know what happened." Charlie looked around. "We need to find something to write on, so we can leave a diary. Maybe when they finally find our bodies—"

"Look, dude, you can't think like that. You have to stay positive." I walked over and slapped his back. "We can do this. We're survivors. How many times have you and I tackled the swamps and survived? Just you and me against the elements. We've always come out on top. We're invincible."

After a long moment of neither of us saying anything, Charlie shook his head. "Poor Brett. I never knew anyone who got killed—like murdered."

"Yeah, that doesn't happen much in Mathport." I sighed. "Well, if it makes you feel any better, his blood is on my hands."

"What do you mean?"

"It's all my fault. It was my stupid idea to come out here and search for Joy. I don't know what I was thinking. What made me think I could do what hundreds of trained people couldn't do?" I plopped to the ground beside Charlie and shook my head. "I dragged y'all into this hell with me, and now Brett's gone—and for what? We're no closer to finding Joy. For all we know, she's dead, too. This was a horrible idea."

We both sat quiet for a long moment. Charlie broke the silence.

"You didn't drag us out here. We both wanted to come. Hell, this was a free vacation for us. I would've never had a chance to come out here if it weren't for you." Charlie nodded his head. "You know, you were right—what you said earlier. We can do this. We're invincible. But we have to plan to be here for the long haul—in case help doesn't come right away. We have to figure out what we'll do about food and shelter."

I punched his shoulder. "Now that's the Charlie I know."

Charlie grabbed his rucksack and dumped it on the ground. "Let's do an inventory, see what supplies we have."

I followed his lead and dumped the contents of my rucksack near his. Together, we had a bag of beef jerky, two cans of peaches, a fork, a light sleeping bag, a small first aid kit, a seventy-five-foot length of half-inch nylon rope, two cans of mosquito spray, a water-damaged camera, saturated posters and maps, and two empty water bottles.

"You have the punch knife, and I have Jezebel," I said, "so we have a couple of weapons for protection."

"But a knife is no match for a gun—or a bear." Charlie walked toward the edge of the forest and began searching the ground. "We need to find a couple of stout sticks that we can sharpen into spears and maybe make a bow and some arrows."

"Good idea." I joined him.

It didn't take long to find two straight sticks that were about six feet long and as thick as my wrist. I went to work on mine, and he worked on his, chopping at one end of it with our knives. When I had fashioned a sharp point on my stick, I stabbed it into the ground and it penetrated the soft mud about six inches.

"This'll work," I said.

Charlie finished his spear soon after and hefted it in his hand. "We're ready for bears, wolves, and whatever else this wilderness has to offer."

"Now we need to prepare for Leaf Creature."

Charlie scrunched his nose. "Bows and arrows like the good old days?"

"Yep. We need to be able to shoot back at it." I searched the ground carpet until I found a green limb that was flexible, but stout enough to serve as a bow. While I did that, Charlie worked on shaving some straight twigs for arrows. I notched both ends of the limb to set the string and then carved finger grooves at the center. Next, I cut three feet of rope, tied a loop at each end, and attached it to the bow. I plucked it when I was done and nodded my approval. "We were built for this kind of life."

"That thing's so tight you could play it like a harp." Charlie grabbed it out of my hands and admired it. "This is better than the ones we built as kids."

"It's a good piece of wood." I surveyed the arrows Charlie had whittled from the straightest branches he could find. "Not bad, but where are the feathers?"

"I'll make a run to Cabela's in a minute," Charlie said.

I laughed and then shrugged. "I guess we'll have to make due. What other choice do we have?"

We placed our weapons on the side and began repacking our rucksacks. I was about to toss the can of mosquito spray in my bag, but stopped and hefted it in my hand. "Dude, I didn't get bit by a single mosquito since we've been here."

Charlie cocked his head sideways. "You're right. I didn't break my spray out once."

I shrugged, then dropped it into my rucksack. "I guess they don't live around here."

"So, what do we do for food?" Charlie asked. "In the long term?"

"We can share your bag of beef jerky for lunch and eat my two cans of peaches for supper."

"And then?"

I didn't know, so I just ignored the question.

"Well, here's lunch…" Charlie tore open the bag of beef jerky and handed me a few pieces. Grateful for the savory shreds of dried meat, I took my time chewing each one, knowing it might be the last piece of meat I would eat in a long time—maybe even the rest of my life. As soon as the thought entered my mind, I dismissed it. I had to stay positive. In boxing, if you became discouraged, you started making mistakes and you could get knocked out. You had to stay positive, no matter how bad your circumstances were. The stakes were much higher in our situation, so that meant it was even more important we stayed positive.

After I'd eaten the last of my beef jerky, I stretched and pulled my rucksack over my shoulders. My back didn't ache as much as it had the day before and I was grateful. Charlie was still chewing on his beef jerky when we set off again. He carried a spear in each hand and I carried the bow and three arrows.

I led the way and began counting my paces again. Each time we approached a bend in the river, I held my breath, hoping we would find some sign of human life when we rounded the curve, even while fearing we'd run into Leaf Creature. And each time, I blew the air out in frustration when we encountered nothing but more of the same and sighed in relief that we didn't encounter that creep.

We kept walking until the sun was well into its western slide behind the distant mountains. An hour earlier, I had begun looking for the perfect spot to camp for the night, and I finally found it. Some large rocks lined the opposite riverbank and just beyond the rocks a giant concave was carved into the side of the mountain. A number of boulders were positioned at the entrance to the concaved area and would offer excellent protection from marauding animals and would keep us out of sight of Leaf Creature, if he was tracking us.

"Look there." I pointed. "That's the perfect camp. It'll keep us dry if it rains, and those giant boulders should shield us from any wild animals lurking around and give us cover if we have to fight Leaf Creature."

Charlie tromped across the river and climbed over the rocks. I followed him. When we entered the concave area, I realized it was cut deeper into the mountain than I'd first thought. It looked like a shallow cave.

"This is bigger than I thought," I said. "And there's no way a falling tree can get to us in here."

"You're right, Abe. I like it. It's dry and secure—like a fort." He looked around. "If only we could make a fire."

"Building a giant fire right at the middle of the opening would definitely keep us safe from wild animals, but it might attract Leaf Creature."

"I think those rocks will block out the light," Charlie said. "Besides, I'd feel much better with fire. More secure."

"I agree." I dropped my rucksack and dug through it until I found the rope. Palming Jezebel, I cut a two-foot piece.

"What're you doing?" Charlie asked.

"See if you can find some dry twigs, leaves, and pine needles.

I'm going to try something I saw in a hunting magazine."

Charlie did as I asked, and I walked along the riverbank until I found a solid piece of tree bark, a flexible stick about eighteen inches long, and another stick about a foot long. I placed the tree bark on the ground near the opening to our new home and carved out a small notch in the center of it. I pointed to it. "Put the leaves and pine needles there."

Charlie dropped a handful of dried and cracking leaves on the bark around the notch. I carved a blunt tip on one end of the foot-long stick and set it aside. I then made a small bow out of the eighteen-inch stick.

"You making a kid bow?" Charlie asked.

"Not quite." I picked up the foot-long stick, placed it alongside my bow and twisted the rope around the foot-long stick. I was almost ready to get to work. I looked around.

"What do you need?" Charlie asked.

"A piece of flat rock."

Charlie walked around and quickly came up with one. "Here."

I placed the tip of the foot-long stick into the notch on the solid bark, secured the top of the stick with the flat rock, and began sawing back and forth with my bow. With each stroke of the bow, the foot-long stick spun like a top and the tip rubbed against the notch, causing friction. I sawed vigorously. Back and forth. Faster and faster. My arm burned, my hand ached, but still I sawed. I grew excited when I saw a puff of smoke start to rise from the bark.

"You're getting it!" Charlie shouted. "Keep going."

I sawed even faster, spurred on by hope. "Blow on it!"

Charlie dropped his face close to the pine needles and began blowing softly. The smoke drifted away with his breath. My arm screamed. I felt the bow starting to slow. I grunted as I sawed through the pain. The pain faded to numbness, and my arm stopped obeying me. It started to slow down on its own and the bow slipped clumsily out of my hand, falling to the rocky ground. I stood and shook out my arm, groaning as a million molten needles pierced the underside of my skin.

"No," Charlie shouted. "No! Why'd you stop? We were almost there."

"My arm just quit." I tried to rub away the pain, but it wasn't working.

Charlie snatched up the bow and fumbled with the flat rock and the foot-long stick. He tried his best to keep the tip of the stick in the notch and get into a rhythm, but it was no use. "How do you do this?"

Feeling was starting to seep back into my hands. "It's not as easy as it looks."

Charlie nodded and, after several futile minutes of trying, tossed the bow to the side. "What's the name of that hunting magazine?"

I shook my head. "I don't remember."

"Find out because when we get back home, I'm suing them."

I couldn't help but laugh. Charlie had gone to my rucksack and removed the two cans of peaches. He tossed one toward me. I reached for it with my right hand, but it bounced off my stomach as my arm refused to move as fast as I told it to. I picked it up with my left hand and took a seat on a smooth rock. I cursed myself for not buying the large cans of fruit, then popped the top off. I dumped the contents in my mouth and ate it all in one gulp. After swallowing the sweet fruit and drinking the juices, I tossed the can near my rucksack.

Charlie turned his empty can upside down and stared at it. "That's the last of our food."

I walked outside and looked downriver. The thick forest made it difficult to see for any great distance, but there was a sliver of an opening where the river cut through the mountains and I could see sharp peaks accentuated against the orange glow in the western sky.

"The river leads west," I said.

"Yeah, earlier the sun was to our back, and then on our left, and our right. This river curves more than my sister's hair." Charlie frowned, staring off in the distance. "I never thought I'd say this, but I really miss that little redheaded brat."

"So much so that you regret telling her she was adopted? Or that she's not a real person because she's got red hair? Or that your mom and dad tried to sell her for a glass of whiskey when she was little, but nobody wanted her?"

Charlie's face lit up and he began laughing. It was the first time I'd seen him happy since yesterday, and it made me feel good. "No, I don't regret any of it. Seriously, she used to scare the crap out of me when she was little. That little snot would be crawling around the house making strange noises, drooling everywhere, and she'd stare at me with this strange look on her face.

"I used to think her drool was venom and that she was trying to poison me with it because she would always follow me around, trying desperately to get her spit on me. She had some evil intent going on in that noggin of hers. I'd even lock my door at night because I was afraid she'd catch me in my sleep."

"I'd be scared, too." I stopped for a second and forced myself to imagine we weren't lost, Brett wasn't dead, Joy wasn't missing, and we had all the food we could eat. If that were the case, this would be an awesome place—it would be paradise. I turned to Charlie. "We're staying here."

He looked confused. "What do you mean?"

"We're no more than a day from the trail. If we're walking in the wrong direction, we'll just keep traveling away from civilization and deeper into the wilderness. We should camp here during the night and scout the area during the day to see if there're any cabins nearby and to see if we can run into the search party."

"What search party?" Charlie asked.

"I'm sure they know we're missing by now," I said.

"How would they know that—for sure?" Charlie challenged.

"Because the last time my dad heard from us was Saturday night. He's definitely called it in by now."

Charlie folded his arms across his chest. "Do you remember Space Camp?"

I scowled. "You didn't even know me when I went to Space Camp."

"I didn't have to. Your mom tells that story to everyone who'll listen. How they dropped you off at Space Camp when you were nine with instructions to call every night, but you never called once. You think they expect anything different from you at seventeen? Sorry, buddy, but they won't start looking for us until we don't show up at the end of the week. We're on our own for at least four more days."

Although I didn't like his assessment, I couldn't argue. I nodded toward the cave. "This is the best shelter we've seen yet. I think we should stay here and wait for the search party that will eventually come for us. If we keep walking, we may be outrunning them—and we stand a good chance of running into Leaf Creature. Out there, we're vulnerable, but here, we've got a fighting chance. What do you think?"

"We need food, and if we don't get it soon, we'll die before they even start looking for us."

"We'll get food," I said with more confidence than I felt.

"How?"

"I'll think of something." The orange glow in the distance was slowly fading to black. I turned into the cave, which was much darker now. "Let's get settled into our new home before it's too dark to see."

Charlie and I placed our rucksacks on the ground next to each other and kept our spears close by. We stretched out and stared up into the blackness above us. I closed my eyes and felt my muscles begin to relax. It felt nice to be able to sleep and not worry about waking up with a giant tree on top of me or a bear eating my leg—

Rocks rattled somewhere toward the river's edge and stirred me from my semi-unconsciousness.

"Abe," Charlie asked, his voice a hoarse whisper.

"What?" I opened my eyes, couldn't see a thing.

"You don't think this is a bear's den or Leaf Creature's cave, do you?"

CHAPTER 12

I jerked to a seated position. More rocks crunched out by the river, getting louder, which meant it was getting closer. Whatever it was, it sounded really big.

"Abe, that's the man! He's here to kill us."

I reached around in the dark for the bow, but couldn't find it. I felt the spear, so I snatched it up. I opened my eyes wide and even squinted, but it was no use. I couldn't see a thing. "Can you see it?"

"What do we do?" Charlie asked in a hushed tone. "Should we attack him? Should we wait for him to come in? What should we do?"

I gripped my spear and pointed it toward where I heard the noise. The rattling of rocks moved even closer. When it reached the opening to the cave, it stopped. I could hear heavy breathing. My heart raced.

"We've got to do something, Abe."

"Do you have the bow?"

"No."

"Grab some rocks," I whispered, trying to sound sure of myself. "On three, yell as loud as you can and throw the rocks toward that breathing sound."

"Okay," Charlie said.

I rested the spear on my knees, where I could easily retrieve it, and then felt around for some rocks. I dragged half a dozen softball-sized rocks next to me, held two of them in my left hand and clutched one in my right hand. I began counting slowly and quietly, "One…two…*three!*"

I screamed bloody murder and chunked the rock as hard as I

could toward the opening of the cave. I heard a muffled *thump* as my rock hit something soft. There was a startled animalistic grunt and a violent rustling of loose rocks. It was a bear!

Charlie screamed like a banshee beside me—scaring me half to death—and I heard another thump as his rock hit the mark. As fast as my hands could move, I launched my other two rocks toward the cave opening, yelling like a man possessed. The grunting wails of a startled animal grew fainter as it rushed off. I whooped and hollered, jumping up and down with confidence.

"We did it," Charlie said. "It worked!"

I couldn't see Charlie, but I could hear him jumping around, and I imagined he was doing a victory dance in the dark.

"What about that scream?" I asked, after I had settled down and my heart had slowed to a normal beat. "You sounded like a little girl who walked into a room full of cockroaches."

"What happens in the cave stays in the cave," Charlie said.

I laughed. "If it takes you getting in touch with your feminine side to scare off bears, knock yourself out. I'll proudly call you Charlene, my best female friend."

"Watch it, pal."

Snatching my spear from the ground, I picked my way carefully through the cave until I was standing in the open air. To my surprise, things were brighter than inside the cave. The moon shone off the water and cast an eerie glow along the riverbanks. I was able to make out the light tones of the surrounding rocks against the shadowy background of the trees.

"Hey, there's moonlight out here," I said.

Charlie joined me. "It's nice to see you again."

"Likewise, my fearless warrior companion."

Spears in hand, we scanned the area. Far off in the distance, we could hear the large animal making its escape, snapping twigs as it crashed through the underbrush.

"That was definitely a bear," I said.

"Unless…"

"Unless what?"

"You don't think that could've been Leaf Creature, do you?"

"Nope. Not at all." The hair on my neck stood up at the thought of being wrong and I changed the subject. "We need to find food, Charlie. If not, we'll die."

"We also need fire to keep animals out of our house. If we'd both been sleeping when that bear came knocking, we could've wakened up dead. From now on, until we figure out how to make fire, we need to sleep in shifts."

"I believe you're right. Rock, paper, scissors?"

Charlie sighed and reentered the cave. "Okay, okay—if you insist. I'll take first sleep while you keep us safe."

I started to protest, then thought better of it. I turned to face the cave. I could hear Charlie moving about inside, but I couldn't see him or even detect a hint of movement, which made me feel a little better about Leaf Creature—he couldn't shoot what he couldn't see. But bears—they could sniff us out in the dark. I shuddered when I thought that a bear had been standing right where I was standing and had been watching us sleep. I knew I'd have to work harder on the fire sticks the next day. Without it, we wouldn't be able to properly defend ourselves.

I walked to the opening of the cave and felt around until I found a smooth rock to lean against. I sat down, stretched my legs, and placed my spear in my lap. After a minute, I quickly pulled Jezebel from her sheath and held her in my right hand. I would've traded her for a rifle, but the cold steel felt good in my hand and gave me some comfort. I made small talk with myself, sang as many country songs as I could remember, recited every joke I'd ever heard, counted backward from a hundred thousand…

*   *   *

My face was warm. There was an orange glow through my eyelids. I opened my eyes and glanced lazily around. It was daylight. Jezebel was on the ground next to me. My spear was still in my lap. I looked over my shoulder into the cave. Charlie was curled in a fetal position snoring. I grunted.

Thank God that bear didn't come back while I was sleeping. It would've killed us both in our sleep.

I clambered to my feet, rubbed the sleep from my eyes, and walked to the riverbank. I longed for a toothbrush. Dropping to my knees, I sucked water into my mouth and swished it around. I spat the water into the sand beside me. I then used my finger to brush my teeth and rinsed my mouth out again. My hair and face felt greasy. I pinched my nose and submerged my whole head under the water. When the icy liquid wrapped its freezing fingers around me, I jerked my head back and gasped.

"Whew! That was cold." Wide awake now, I returned to the cave. Before we did anything else, we needed to figure out how to get food and we had to make a fire.

Charlie was sitting up when I entered the cave. "Where'd you go?"

"I washed my face in the river." I collected my fire-making kit and walked to the edge of the cave opening and placed it on the ground.

"Trying that again?" Charlie asked.

"I have to." I placed the tinder near the notch in the bark, set the foot-long in the notch and began sawing away with the bow. The muscles in my arm ached from the night before, and I didn't know if I'd have the endurance to produce a spark. I must have sawed for ten minutes and still didn't get so much as a puff of smoke. Sweat was now forming on my forehead. I paused to wipe my face with the short sleeve of my shirt. I glanced over at Charlie. He was sitting cross-legged on a large slab of rock, bent over, staring intently at something on the rock. He would press a finger to the rock, rub it onto his shorts, and then continue scanning the rock.

"What're you doing?" I asked.

"Playing King of the Rock," Charlie said absently.

"Doing what?"

"My rock is being attacked by ants. I'm trying to protect it."

"Maybe you could do something productive. Like getting out there and finding some food."

"Remember when we used to burn ants with a magnifying glass?" Charlie asked, not a bit fazed by my suggestion.

"Yep, I do. What about finding some food, there, buddy?"

Charlie kept smashing the defenseless ants. "I sure wish I had a magnifying glass right now."

I grunted and turned back to sawing. I was bent into my work and sawing like a wild man when a thought suddenly occurred to me. It was so profound I dropped the bow. I turned to Charlie. "Charlie, I've got it!"

Startled, he looked up. "You made fire?" He looked at the pile of tinder that still rested on the bark. It was unmarred. "It doesn't look like you've got fire, so what do you got?"

I dashed into the cave and dragged Charlie's rucksack into the light.

"What're you doing?" Charlie's curiosity fully aroused, he abandoned his attack on the ants. "Do you think I've got food hidden in there? You think I'm holding out on you? What kind of friend do you think I am?"

I ripped the bag open and dug around until I found the camera. I pressed the release button and twisted the lens off, then tossed the camera back in the bag. Charlie's eyes widened and his mouth formed a large "O" as he suddenly understood.

"I get it," he said.

"Grab more leaves and twigs."

Charlie snapped into action, and I moved my fire-making kit into the sunlight. I held the lens about a foot over the ground and turned it until it captured the sunlight and shot a beam down on the bark. I adjusted the height of the lens until it focused the sunlight like a thin laser and then I guided the beam over the tinder. Within seconds, the tinder began to smoke and soon after, it burst into flames. With hands that shook, I snatched up nearby twigs and placed them on top of the tinder. The tiny flame licked hungrily at the twigs and grew in intensity. Warm air rose from the flames and caressed my face. I leapt into the air like I'd done when I'd scored my first knockout in the ring.

"We've got fire!"

Charlie approached at a stumbling run, his arms loaded with twigs and branches. His face lit up and matched the glow from the fire. He dropped the firewood, grabbed me in a bear hug and tried to lift me off the ground. He couldn't, so he released me and just jumped up and down and screamed, "You did it! You're the man!"

"No," I said, "it was you. When you started talking about the magnifying glass, it got me thinking. *You're* the man."

As the fire grew stronger, Charlie and I continued fueling it. We scrambled up and down the mountainside around the cave and deposited armload after armload of branches just inside the cave, where they would be safe from any rain that might come. There were a number of trees that had fallen sometime in the distant past. With swift kicks, I was able to snap off large branches and drag them to the cave. When we thought we had enough firewood to last several days, we sank to the rocks. Exhausted and hungry, we lay there for several minutes trying to catch our breath.

"I need food," Charlie said.

We both did. While we were in no danger of starving to death just then, we needed energy to defend ourselves against any marauding animals and Leaf Creature—if it came to that. I stood. My head swam, and I swayed slightly. I shook my head to clear it, snatched up Charlie's empty rucksack and pulled it onto my shoulders.

"Keep the fire going," I said and walked off.

"Where you going?"

I pulled Jezebel from her sheath. "I'm going kill some lunch."

"I'm coming."

I raised my hand to stop him. "Someone needs to tend the fire to make sure it doesn't go out. If it goes out and we lose sunlight, we're screwed."

Charlie looked around at the surrounding forest. "What about Leaf Creature?"

"I'll take my spear with me, just in case."

"I wasn't talking about you."

"You've got the other spear and the bow and arrows." I pointed to the large rocks that guarded the opening to the cave. "If that creep comes here, just stay behind those rocks. You'll be fine. Stick a long branch in the fire in case a wild animal comes around—you can stick that flame in their face and they'll leave you alone."

"Just hurry back."

Rotating my head like it was on a swivel, I searched my surroundings as I walked downriver. When I'd gone about a hundred yards, I came upon a section of forest that was clear of underbrush. I took a right and tromped through the thick leafy blanket that covered the forest floor. I scanned the tree branches overhead. There were plenty of birds flapping around. They would land on a branch momentarily and then fly off to another branch. They never stayed in one place long enough for me to zero in with my knife. Even if I could, I didn't know if I should try, because if I missed, Jezebel would go sailing off into the air and I might never find her again.

As I walked, the mountain began to angle downward and I soon found myself at the edge of a large meadow cloaked with knee-high grass. A number of trees grew in spots along the meadow and I thought I saw something hanging from the branches on one of them. I waded through the grass and nearly yelped when I reached the trees and saw dozens of fat green pears. I shrugged the rucksack off my shoulders and began filling it with the fruit.

I paused to take a huge bite from one of them. The sweet juices flowed smoothly down my throat. When I was done with the first one, I dropped it and reached for another, but movement to my left caught my eye. I turned and froze. A huge mother bear and three cubs were walking directly toward me. They were about fifty yards away. I clutched the rucksack and began backing slowly away from the tree. The mother bear saw me and stopped, then stood on her hind legs. I continued backing away and didn't stop until I reached the tree line. After determining I wasn't a threat, the mother bear led her cubs to the tree, stood on her hind legs and pulled pears down for the cubs to eat. One of the cubs took a loping start, jumped onto the tree trunk and scaled effortlessly up it.

I turned to walk away and another movement caught my eyes at the edge of the meadow. I dropped to my knees and studied the area. There was nothing. Fear paralyzed me. When we had first encountered Leaf Creature, it had been impossible to see it if it didn't move. It had blended perfectly into the background. *Is that Leaf Creature? Is this the way it ends for me?*

The movement happened again, and I sighed in relief. It was a rabbit. I quickly gauged the distance—twenty feet. Without thought, I palmed Jezebel and launched her through the air. One of the blades entered the rabbit just below the neck and killed it instantly. Keeping a wary eye on the four bears, I hurried to the rabbit, retrieved Jezebel, and snatched up the soft furry animal. It was much thicker than any rabbit I'd hunted in Louisiana. It must've weighed ten or fifteen pounds. I stuffed it into the rucksack and headed back to camp.

It was the first time I'd killed anything with my throwing knife other than a snake, and I was secretly proud. I'd set out to get lunch and succeeded. I'd taken on the Great Blue Summit Mountains and won. We had fire and we had food. We could survive until the search party found us—unless Leaf Creature found us first.

CHAPTER 13

"Hello the camp," I hollered when the cave came into view, copying a phrase I'd learned from reading Dad's old Louis L'Amour westerns. Charlie had clearly been busy. He had started another smaller fire inside the cave, where the weather couldn't get to it. He had stored a large amount of firewood deep inside the cave. He had stacked a number of stones on either side of the larger fire and positioned two long thin slabs of rock across the fire to serve as a grill. "Wow, Charlie, you've been busy."

Charlie looked up. His face fell. "You didn't find anything for lunch? I thought you'd bring back a deer or something."

I dropped the heavy rucksack to the ground and snatched a pear from inside and tossed it to him. I could've sworn he took a bite out of it while it was still in the air.

"God, this is good. Where'd you find it?" Pear juice dripped down Charlie's chin, but he didn't seem to notice.

"In a meadow down the river and to the right. There must be a dozen pear trees out there. We should be set for a while." I pulled out the rabbit and held it up like a trophy. "There are also some of these running around."

"Whoa! He's huge," Charlie said.

I nodded. "Do you mind cleaning it and cooking it?"

"Cook it? How? I don't know how to cook a peanut butter and jelly sandwich, much less a rabbit."

"And I do?" I waved him off. "It can't be that hard. Just skin it, shove a stick up its butt, and suspend it over the fire until the meat's tender."

"Sounds good to me. What about you? What're you doing?"

"I want to cross the river and hike about a mile that way"—I pointed directly across from us—"to see if I can come upon a trail. If we find a trail, we find our way out of here."

Charlie frowned.

"I know what you're thinking," I said. "I'll be fine. I'll stick to the wide open areas where no one can sneak up behind me."

"Okay." Charlie pulled out the punch knife I'd given him and grabbed the rabbit by the tail. "Lunch will be done by the time you get back."

I grabbed my spear and shoved a pear in each of the side pockets on my cargo shorts, just in case I got hungry. Taking great care not to slip on the green slime that coated most of the rocks in the river, I picked my way to the other side. The riverbank was elevated and I had to climb a short cliff to reach the forest floor. Although the trees were spread out and there was no dense underbrush, the forest was dark and shadowy. Holding my spear at the ready and scanning my surroundings, I made my way deeper into the woodlands. I tried to avoid making too much noise, but it was hard to walk stealthily in the dried leaves that covered the ground.

Every now and then, I heard rustling in the leaves and I would freeze. I couldn't always detect the origin of the sounds, but I caught a glimpse of a number of squirrels scurrying through the dry leaves. I'd never eaten squirrel, but if I got a bead on one, it would end up on the stick. I saw about a dozen deer through the trees, but I couldn't get close to them. Even if I could, I was afraid Jezebel might not kill them and they would run off with her.

I paced off what I thought was a mile-and-a-half, but I never came upon anything resembling a trail and the terrain never changed, so I turned and headed back toward camp.

As I walked, I had an eerie feeling I was being watched. I looked over my shoulder often, trying to penetrate the depths of the shadows, searching for Leaf Creature or anything else that would explain my apprehension—I was praying it was "anything else." Just to be safe, I quickened my step and was able to make much better time on the return trip. I was relieved when the smell of freshly roasted meat greeted my nostrils and the river's whitecaps came into view through the trees. I hurried along the last stretch of the forest—glad to be out of the darkness—and slid down the small cliff. I splashed back across the river, and Charlie was pulling the rabbit from the stick when I reached the camp.

"It smells good, Chef Rickman."

Charlie looked up from where he was slicing the meat off the bones. "I couldn't find any salt in your bag, so I just sweated all over it."

I leaned my spear against the cave entrance and took my seat on one of the rocks. I examined the strips of rabbit meat. "It looks like chicken."

Charlie reached behind his seat and handed me a smooth slab of stone. "It's not fine china, but it'll have to do."

"You thought of everything, didn't you?"

"I ordered up two Cokes, but they didn't get here yet, so I don't know what we're going to drink."

We had fire, but nothing to boil the water in. I shrugged. "I'd rather get sick than die of thirst."

"I'd rather have the Coke," Charlie said.

I retrieved the two empty water bottles we'd been carrying and filled them in the river. I held the bottles up to the sunlight. They looked crystal clear. "Looks fine," I said and handed Charlie a bottle.

Charlie had divided the rabbit into equal portions. I grabbed what was mine and began eating the slivers of meat. It seemed like forever since I'd eaten hot food. Although it wasn't flavored, I was positive it was the best meat I'd ever eaten. While the rabbit had seemed huge when I killed it, the amount of meat it produced wasn't indicative of its size, and I wondered if it would be enough to fill our bellies. Between bites of rabbit, I ate the pears I'd stuffed into my pockets earlier. Before long, I could no longer feel hunger pangs and I even felt a little stuffed.

"God, that was good," I said.

Charlie was finishing his and nodded. "Worst rabbit I ever ate, but it tasted better than the best rabbit I ever ate."

I slid off the rock and sat flat on the ground, using the rock as a backrest. I stretched my legs and allowed my eyes to slip shut for a minute. "If I didn't know better, I'd think we were living the dream."

"I don't even care if we're never found now," Charlie said. "We have food, water, shelter, fire, and a beautiful backyard. What more could a man ask for?"

I opened my eyes and stiffened up. "And pets."

Charlie turned to where I was looking. A monster black bear was making his way across the river, walking straight for us. He would take a couple of steps, pause as the rushing water sprayed foam against his jet black fur, test the wind with his nostrils, and then continue toward us. He didn't look scared of us or the fire. Before I could do anything Charlie had sprung up and made a mad dash for the deepest recesses of the cave.

"Get in here, Abe," Charlie yelled. "That bear means business."

Remembering what I'd read, I stood on top of the rock and waved my arms high into the air and let out a war cry. It was so loud I even scared myself a little, but the bear didn't hesitate. He continued coming toward me like he'd been commanded to do so. Everything I'd read told me to stand my ground, so I snatched up my spear and screamed as loud as I could. My throat ached from the strain. The bear was only a dozen feet away—and closing fast—when I stabbed at it with the edge of my spear. The tip of the spear poked the left side of his shoulder, but he didn't even flinch. He walked right through it and pawed angrily at my leg.

My heart raced. I jumped off the rock and backed away. My body trembled. A wooden arrow shot right passed me and ricocheted off the bear's furry shoulder. The bear made grunting noises and continued forward.

Desperate, I screamed and swung the spear at his head, but the stick glanced off his thick skull. Letting out a terrifying growl, the bear lunged forward. I jumped back, tripped on a loose rock, and landed hard on my left shoulder. I scrambled to my feet. I don't know when I drew her, but Jezebel seemed to just appear in my hand. The bear swatted at my face with his left paw. I covered up with my right forearm and took the full brunt of the blow on the arm. Although the paw hadn't hit my head, the sheer force of the blow was enough to rattle my teeth and send me flying to the side. I scrambled backward on my butt, eyes wide, focused on the bear. I continued moving until my back smashed into a tree and stopped me dead in my tracks. I gasped. The bear was stalking straight for me. This was it—I was dead.

I dragged myself to my feet and leaned against the tree. I held Jezebel out in front of me for one last stand. From the corner of my eye, I saw Charlie approaching stealthily from the bear's right flank, spear in hand. He was too far away. The bear would be on me before Charlie could get within striking distance. I could almost smell its breath and braced myself for what was about to happen, ready to plunge Jezebel deep into the beast's throat. If only I could hold it off long enough—

All of a sudden, the bear stopped and dropped his head, almost at my feet. There, spread all over the dry leaves and branches, were the entrails and what was left of the rabbit carcass. The bear began wolfing it down as though I didn't even exist. I almost wet my pants as I crept around to the opposite side of the tree. I then backed deeper into the forest and gave the bear a wide berth as I made my way back to the cave. Once there, I collapsed to my knees near the fire, shaking. I kept a close watch on the bear as I knelt there.

Charlie's eyes were wide. His mouth opened and closed several times, but nothing came out. He pointed down at my arm, gulped, and finally got out, "You...you're bleeding."

I glanced down at my forearm. There were three deep gashes on the outside of my right arm. Blood gushed from the lacerations to drip on the rocky ground. I saw a thin line of yellow fat under the skin. I grimaced.

"I need to close those wounds before you bleed to death." Charlie rushed to his bag and returned with his first aid kit.

I kept glancing toward the bear. He finished eating all the rabbit's body parts and then polished the rocks with his tongue. When he was done, he turned and ambled away, crossing the river and disappearing into the forest as though he hadn't just tried to kill someone.

I stood on uncertain legs, real fear gripping my chest and constricting my breathing. I stumbled forward until I was standing over where the rabbit's body parts had been.

"Get back here," Charlie said.

"You've got to see this, Charlie."

Charlie exited the cave with the first aid kit in hand and walked to where I stood. "Come sit down so I can clean your—"

"Look at those rocks. There's absolutely no evidence a rabbit was ever here. Not even a drop of blood."

Charlie shrugged. "So? Maybe he was hungry."

"If that bear kills us and eats us, they'll never find any trace of us. No one would ever know what happened to us. We wouldn't be able to tell them about Brett. We'd just be like the others—gone without a trace."

"Let's not worry about that now," Charlie said. "You're dripping blood all over the rocks and that's liable to attract more bears."

Charlie pressed a piece of white gauze against my forearm and held it in place while guiding me toward the campfire. I followed reluctantly and sat on one of the large rocks. Charlie twisted the cap off a small bottle of alcohol and held it over my cuts.

"Get ready," he said. "This'll burn like the devil."

I gritted my teeth, nodded for him to deliver the pain. Giving no thought to waste, Charlie splashed a healthy dose of the alcohol onto my cuts. I inadvertently gasped when I felt the burn. Sweat appeared on my forehead. The pain was so deep and searing it felt like it had penetrated my bones. Having endured a great deal of pain already in my short life—from fighting three rounds with a broken hand to getting my broken nose beat on for four rounds to ripping a thumbnail off during a grappling session—I appreciated the intensity of the burn.

"Do you want me to blow on it?" Charlie asked.

I shook my head. "Let me savor it. As long as I can still feel the pain I know I'm alive."

"Dude, you're just sick with your pain stuff." Charlie tossed the bottle of alcohol back in the kit and then grabbed a tube of antibiotic cream. After squirting a healthy dose of the cream over the cuts, he pulled out more gauze. "This won't be enough to wrap half your cuts."

"I have that sleeping bag—it's more of a blanket. Get it and cut a strip about this long"—I held my hands about three feet apart—"and you can tie it off to try and stop the bleeding."

Charlie pulled the sleeping bag from my rucksack and began cutting it into strips.

"Hey, you just need one," I said.

"For now, but we'll need to change the dressing often so you don't get some kind of crazy infection." Charlie was able to make a dozen strips of bandage. He stowed away eleven of them and returned to me with one. Using some of the stuffing he'd removed from the sleeping bag, he wiped away the blood and ordered me to hold it over the cuts and elevate my arm.

"How do you know so much about this kind of thing?" I asked, following his orders. "I didn't know you were studying to be a nurse."

"Remember when you used to take fourth-hour PE with all your football buddies?"

I nodded.

"Among the other useless electives I signed up for was first aid class."

"First aid?" I asked. "Why on earth would you take that?"

"I figured it would be an easy A, and I thought I'd get to practice CPR on some hot chicks."

I laughed hysterically. "You didn't think you'd get to practice on a real live girl?"

His face red, Charlie nodded. "Yep, call me stupid, but I really thought that. In fact, I thought it right up until they brought those ridiculous-looking half-bodied dummies into the room. I had even partnered with that Hailey girl."

"From choir?"

"Yep, her."

"She agreed to be your partner?" I asked, a bit skeptical.

Charlie nodded. "I was about to ask her if she wanted to get down on her back first when the teacher broke out those plastic mouthpieces. I thought about bailing right then, but it was too late."

As Charlie finished dressing my arm, I gave some thought to the way the bear had acted. "You know Charlie, that bear wasn't one bit afraid of me."

"Neither would I be if I was that much bigger than you," he said.

I squeezed my fist to test Charlie's wrapping job. Pain shot up my arm. "It had nothing to do with the bear's size. Bears are naturally afraid of humans, but that bear didn't appear to have an ounce of fear."

"What's your point?" Charlie asked.

"Do you know when it is that bears lose their fear of humans?"

"When people start feeding them."

"Exactly right. When people feed bears, it conditions the bears to associate humans with food. Instead of being afraid of people, they start seeking them out. In fact, most of the unprovoked bear attacks I've read about happened when a conditioned bear lost its fear of humans and some unsuspecting person got between him and his food."

Charlie returned the first aid kit to his rucksack and threw several more logs on the fire. "What's that got to do with your bear attack?"

"I think people have been feeding the bear."

Charlie waved his arms around. "But who? We're so deep in the backcountry there aren't even any trails out here." Charlie pointed to a footprint one of us had made earlier. "It's probably the first time this patch of soft mud has ever seen the bottom of a human foot. I think a more likely theory is the bear never saw a human being before and he didn't know he was supposed to be afraid of you."

I shook my head. "Bears are born with a fear of humans. I'd be willing to bet our next three meals people have been feeding it. If I'm right, we're closer to civilization than we thought."

That immediately got Charlie's attention. "You think so?"

"Based on how much noise he made walking through the rocks, I'm betting it's the same bear we heard last night and this area is part of his home range."

"But can't a bear's home range cover up to a hundred miles?"

"Not if the food source is abundant," I said. "Out here, there's so much food I'm betting he doesn't wander more than five to ten miles."

Charlie thought about this for a moment and his eyes lit up. "You think we're five to ten miles away from civilization?"

I nodded.

Charlie walked out to the river. "Then why are we sitting here? Let's get out there and find our way home."

"One of us has to stay here and keep the fire going, just in case I'm wrong." I joined Charlie and pointed across the river. "The bear came from there and then headed up river, so he must be getting food from one of those places."

"But I thought you already scouted the area across the river?"

"I only went a mile-and-a-half. I'm betting if we take turns traveling five miles in all directions we'll run into civilization." I turned back toward the cave. "Let's get a good night's sleep and then I'll take the first trip. I'll head back across the—"

"You took the first trip today," Charlie said. "I want to go next, but I want to head behind the cave. I feel like we'll connect with some trails there."

"Sounds good. While you're gone, I'll keep the fires going and do a little hunting close by."

Charlie and I cleaned off the cooking area and the slabs of rock that served as our plates. Each time I picked up something with my right arm the ripped flesh would stretch and the pain would intensify. I couldn't help but wonder if it would interfere with my aim tomorrow while hunting. If it did, we would be in trouble. I'd never practiced throwing left-handed, and Charlie couldn't hit water with a knife if he dropped it in the ocean.

As though reading my mind, Charlie asked, "Hey, can you still hunt with your arm ripped in half like that?"

"Absolutely," I said. "This is nothing but a scratch."

When we were done cleaning up, we settled into the cave and made small talk while we waited for the sun to set. Just as night was falling, Charlie removed my old dressing by the light of the inside fire. "I want to clean it out to make sure it doesn't get infected," Charlie said.

"Yes, Mom."

Charlie poured more alcohol on the deep cuts and it burned more than the first time. When the antibiotic cream had been applied and the new bandage was in place, we settled down for the night. Every now and then, one of us would get up and toss another log on the fire and then settle back on our rucksack. The orange glow cast eerie shadows around the cave.

"You know what would go good right now?" I asked, staring up at the ghosts dancing on the jagged ceiling.

"What's that?"

"A horror story." I went on to tell a story Dad had told me as a kid, but Charlie wouldn't be outdone.

"I've got a story that's scarier than that," Charlie said. "And do you know why?"

"Why's that?" I asked.

"Because it's true."

Charlie went on to tell the story about my earlier bear attack, except he inserted himself as the hero who killed the marauding bear and ate on it for a year. Somewhere along the way, as he went on to describe his many wild mountain adventures, I slipped into a deep slumber.

CHAPTER 14

I woke up early the next morning shivering. I looked over at the fires. Both of them had burned down to coals. I pushed off the ground and winced when the pain in my right arm reminded me about the bear attack. I tried to rub the cold out of my arms as I walked to the pile of firewood and fed both fires. The embers were so hot the branches burst into flames and immediately warmed the inside of the cave. I tossed a couple of big logs onto the fire and sat close, allowing the warmth to hug me like a loving mother who hadn't seen her son in many days.

Charlie woke up soon after I did and pulled on his T-shirt and shoes. I grabbed a couple of pears from our stash and handed him one.

"Thanks." Charlie took a bite and his eyes half closed as he chewed it. "I'm glad you found these."

"I'll run over and get some more later on, so we don't run out."

Charlie studied my face. "Are you hot?"

I shook my head. "I'm actually freezing."

"Your face is red."

Charlie walked over and reached a hand toward my face, but I brushed it away.

"What're you doing?" I wanted to know.

"Checking to see if you have a fever." Charlie touched the back of his hand to my forehead. "You feel hot."

"I'm fine, *Mother*."

Charlie went to the river and filled my bottle of water, dug a Tylenol out of the first aid kit, and handed them to me. "Take this. It'll help keep your fever under control."

I tossed the pill into my mouth and swallowed it down with a gulp of cold river water. I then sat patiently while Charlie changed my bandage.

"We have to get you to a hospital," Charlie said. "You really need some stitches."

"Sure, I'll just call nine-one-one." I laughed and waved him off. "I'll be fine."

Charlie stuffed a couple of pears and a bottle of water into his rucksack. "I'll be back in a few hours. If the chills don't go away, take another Tylenol."

"I've got it, Nurse Charlie." I watched Charlie walk out the cave and disappear around the left corner. When the crunching of his footsteps had faded away, I crept back to my rucksack and sank onto it. I felt weak, tired, and cold.

*   *   *

I didn't know how long I'd slept, but when I woke up, I was sweating. The fires had burned down again. A gentle breeze was blowing and had found its way into the cave. I stretched—winced when I was reminded of my wounds—and dragged myself to my feet. The Tylenol had definitely helped because I no longer felt as weak. Deciding not to deplete our supply of firewood, I ventured out into the forest around the cave and gathered up some dry branches and tossed them into both fires. When they were roaring again, I grabbed my spear and rucksack and headed downriver toward what I'd dubbed Pear Meadow.

When I arrived, the bears were everywhere. There must've been a dozen of them. Some were grazing on berries in the tall grass and some were feeding on the pear trees. I leaned against a tall hardwood and tried to decide what to do. We needed more pears. There were only about five or six left and they would be gone by that evening. I thought about screaming and throwing rocks at the bears, but my last encounter had given me a healthy fear for those wild creatures.

I skirted the edges of the meadow—careful not to make noise and attract attention—and set off into the forest on the opposite side. It wasn't long before I came to another meadow that was located at the edge of a high cliff. I strolled along the edge of the cliff. It was lined with tall pine trees, and I searched for a way down the steep wall. It was impassable. I turned away from the giant pines and surveyed the meadow. There were no pear trees and I cursed my luck, but only for a minute.

Tall grass and bushes blanketed most of the meadow, and I saw them for a few minutes before I realized what they were—patches of wild blackberry bushes. I hurried to them and began picking the blackberries three and four at a time. Careful not to smash them, I plucked hundreds from the prickly vines and stuffed them into an outside pocket of my bag. A picker would occasionally stick my hand and burn, but I ignored it. While I worked, I sampled the groceries. They were good, but not as good as Mom used to make them. She would place the blackberries in a large bowl and sprinkle a healthy quantity of sugar on top and refrigerate them for several hours. As I bit into the thick juicy berries, I imagined they came from that bowl and thought I could actually taste the sugar.

A noise sounded behind me, and I turned in a panic, reaching for my spear. I was relieved to see a squirrel darting up the side of a pine tree. The tree was huge—about six feet wide. Without giving a thought to what I was doing, I quick-drew Jezebel and threw her directly at the squirrel. I grunted when my slash wounds ripped open again—but that was the good news. To my horror, Jezebel flew completely off course, glanced off a piece of tree bark, and disappeared over the cliff. I rushed to the cliff's edge and dropped to my belly to stare over the side. The trees and underbrush were so thick I couldn't even see the forest floor. Jezebel was gone—and with her, our only chance to kill meat. I turned onto my back and covered my face with my hands.

"You idiot! Why'd you do that?"

I must've stayed there for thirty minutes cursing myself. When I moved to stand up, I winced at the aching in my back. Every joint seemed to scream with pain. I'd felt a light version of this same aching in my bones earlier, but it had subsided soon after I ate that Tylenol. Now it was back with a vengeance. I grabbed my rucksack filled with blackberries and my spear and made the return trip to our camp.

When I arrived at the cave, I sank to the floor inside and closed my eyes. The weakness was returning. The aching in my joints intensified. I shuddered. I felt my forehead with the back of my hand, like Charlie had done earlier. It was burning hot. I thought about getting up to get another Tylenol, maybe splash water on my face. I even visualized myself doing it, but I never moved. Instead, I closed my eyes and slipped into a troubling sleep. I dreamed of monster bears, raging rivers, killer squirrels, Joy, and Leaf Creature. I was caught somewhere between a deep sleep and being awake, much like David Banner felt when he had gotten stuck between being a human and being the Incredible Hulk.

*   *   *

It was dark when I woke up. I was still shivering, and I could feel a tremendous amount of heat emitting from my face, especially when I'd breathe. A familiar smell greeted my nostrils and it took me a while to realize it was fish. I lifted my heavy head and looked toward the cave entrance. The two fires burned bright. In the orange glow, I could see Charlie bending over the makeshift rock grill.

"Charlie, what're you doing?" I asked. The words felt like bricks. They seemed to slip out of my mouth and drop to the ground in front of my face. My neck was tired. I rested my head against the rocky floor and tried calling Charlie's name again. He heard it on my third try.

"Hey, don't try to talk," Charlie said. He walked into the cave and knelt beside me. "You're coming down with a fever again. Here, take this Tylenol and drink this water."

He placed the Tylenol on my tongue and, cradling my head, dumped a stream of water into my mouth. It felt cool and soothing against my dry and cracked lips. I sucked down the water, swallowing the Tylenol with it, but not before the bitter taste made my mouth involuntarily scrunch up. "God, that's awful."

Charlie nodded, and I saw a strange look on his face. Even in the dim glow from the fires I recognized that look. It was the same expression he'd had when his mom walked into his room while we were playing video games two years ago and told him his grandpa—the last living connection to his own dad—was in the hospital on life support. Through the blur, I wondered what had happened that made him look like that.

"Look," Charlie said. "You're going to have to eat something."

I lifted a weak hand and pushed at him, shook my head. "No...food. I'm not...not...hungry."

"Listen, Abe, if we expect to get out of here, you'll have to get your strength up. You have to eat something."

I shook my head, closed my tired eyes and turned over. I drifted in and out of consciousness. I had visions of Charlie fussing over the bandage on my arm...grilled fish on the rock grill...Charlie rubbing a cool wet rag over my face and neck...bears attacking our camp...blackberries and sugar...Leaf Creature shooting at us...my mom crying.

*   *   *

I opened my eyes and the first thing I saw was the jagged ceiling of the cave. It was so well lit I knew it had to be a bright day outside. I sat up. My head spun a little, but the chills were gone. Squinting, I tried to see through the glare of the outdoors. I could make out only shadows at first, but the surrounding rocks and trees finally came into view. And there was Charlie, shirtless and squatting on his heels near the fire. I shook my head to clear it and looked back in his direction. He looked different. Darker than I remembered and maybe more muscular. I rose to my feet and stood still for a second, trying to get my legs under me. Charlie noticed the movement and hurried to me.

"Hey, dude, how do you feel?"

I nodded. "I feel good. A little hungry."

Charlie laughed and helped steady me as I walked to one of the large rocks near the outside fire. "You should be hungry. You haven't eaten much of anything in four days. I was able to force some pear juice and blackberry juice down your throat, but that's about it."

Four days? I sat on the rock. My breath was shallow, my head light. I couldn't believe how tired I was from just walking eight or nine steps. "I've been out for four days?"

"On and off. You never really woke up, like good, but you'd stir a little and talk in your sleep." Charlie smiled, and I could almost see the relief in his face. "You said some crazy stuff."

"Like what?"

"Well, at one point you thought I was your mom and you were telling me not to cry. I tried to explain to you that it was me, Charlie, but you said Charlie was a mountain man now and wouldn't be coming home."

I felt my face heat up and turn red. Since I wasn't running a fever anymore, I knew it had to be embarrassment. "I said that?"

"You also kept saying we had to build a gun to fight Leaf Creature because he was attacking us, but you were calling him Nelson Vincent. You'd sit up in the middle of the night screaming like crazy that Nelson was outside with a gun and that he was going to kill us like he killed Brett and Joy." Charlie shuddered. "It would scare the crap out of me. I mean, one minute you're snoring, and the next minute you're screaming like you're on fire. I'm surprised I didn't have a heart attack or—"

"I don't snore."

Charlie nodded. "Like a thunderstorm."

"I don't remember any of it."

"I won't lie to you...I was scared. You were so delirious and your fever was so high I really thought you were going to die and leave me all alone out here."

"What would you've done with my body?"

"What do you mean?" Charlie asked.

"Would you have buried me? Fed me to the bears? Dumped me in the river? What would you have done?"

"None of the above." Charlie pinched the skin on my upper arm. "You lost a bit of weight, but you could've provided enough meat to keep me alive for at least a week."

I laughed as I scanned the area. "Speaking of food—was I dreaming or did I smell fish?"

"That wasn't a dream. I've been eating fish for a few days now." Charlie stood and walked to the river, knelt and stuck his hand in the water. After feeling around in the water for a few seconds, he grabbed a piece of rope and reeled it in hand-over-hand. When he pulled the other end of the rope out of the water there were five or six live fish attached to it. They flapped around, smashing into each other and kicking up water as they wriggled helplessly at the end of the rope.

"What...where...I don't understand," I said. "How'd you catch them?"

Charlie dropped the fish back into the river and pointed at his shoes. "Remember my safety pins you made fun of?"

I nodded.

"I shaped one of them into a hook and tied it to a shred of that nylon rope you brought with you." Charlie walked to the edge of the forest and picked up a rotten piece of log. He broke it open and pulled a fat grub from inside, held it up. "These little babies make excellent trout bait."

"But won't your shoes fall off?" I asked, laughing.

"Nope, I've got plenty of them." He pointed from one to the other and counted out loud. "One, two, three, four, five, six...seven more. I could have eight fishing poles."

"Got any cooked fish?"

"Who needs fish when we've got these?" Charlie tossed the grub in his mouth and ate it.

I gagged. "Are you for real?"

"They're really good when you get used to them. Heck, the bears love them." He walked to a piece of rock that had a large leaf over it. He pulled it back and exposed a couple of thick slabs of fish meat. "I put a portion aside for you each night, hoping you'd be well enough to eat." He brought me the fish from his latest meal and then retrieved a bottle of water. "Enjoy."

I took a bite of the fish and chewed on it for a full minute before swallowing it. My throat hurt, but I almost didn't notice—the fish was that good. "Charlie, you really are turning into a mountain man." As I took another bite—this one bigger—I glanced at his face to confirm my thoughts. "But you still can't grow a beard."

After I ate, I felt a little stronger. I could tell it was early in the day because the sun was low in the eastern sky, but I had no clue what day it was. "Do you know what day it is?"

Charlie shook his head. "I'm not positive, but I guess it's Sunday, so we've been here for over a week. I'm sure your mom called the cops, the FBI, and the army by now and they're all probably looking for us."

"Have you scouted the area? Seen anyone?"

Charlie nodded. "Yeah, I saw this nice man and lady hiking two days ago. They offered us pizza, Coke, and a helicopter, but I turned them down. I was having too much fun rubbing you down with cold water to leave just yet."

I puckered my eyebrows. "Why on earth would you rub me down with cold water?"

"To keep you from bursting into flames."

"Flames?"

Charlie nodded. "You were that hot. I wouldn't be surprised to find out you suffered some brain damage."

I began thinking back to the last few days, testing my memory. Satisfied my ticker was still calibrated, I said, "So, did you scout the area?"

"I didn't want to leave you alone for very long," Charlie explained, "so I stayed close by. I walked a few hundred yards in all directions."

"And no search party, eh?"

"Would we still be here?" Charlie asked.

"I guess you're right. Look, if you want to head out and do some scouting, feel free. I'm feeling good right now. No more aches, no more fever"—I raised my right arm and flexed my hand several times—"and I don't even feel the pain much in my arm anymore."

Charlie hesitated. "You sure?"

"Dude, I want to get out of here just as bad as you do. The sooner we start scouting the area, the sooner we can find some help."

"Okay, I'll go." Charlie grabbed his spear and rucksack. He started to walk downriver, but paused and turned back to me. "Will you be okay without Jezebel?"

I frowned, reached down and touched the empty sheath on my belt. "I guess so."

"What happened to her anyway?" Charlie moved back toward me

and sat on a rock.

"I don't know."

"When I came back from my hike Wednesday, I found you passed out in the cave, your rucksack full of blackberries, and Jezebel gone."

"Oh, the blackberries." I puckered my brow, trying to think back. There had been a second meadow, blackberry bushes, and—oh yeah, that squirrel. "Now I remember. I threw Jezebel at a squirrel and missed. She flew over a cliff and fell pretty far. I looked to see if I could get it, but it was too far down."

"A cliff?" Charlie was suddenly alert. "Could it be the cliff we were on that first day? By that big river?"

"I'm not sure. I didn't see a river at the bottom and nothing in the area looked familiar."

"Where'd you find it?" Charlie asked.

I pointed in the direction he was headed. "Go down the river about a hundred yards and take a right. It'll be right where the forest becomes clear of underbrush. Head straight into the forest from the right side of the river and it'll be the second meadow you come to. But be careful. Oh, and Charlie."

"Yeah?"

"What about Leaf Creature? Any sign of him?"

Charlie shook his head. "Not a peep. I think he's gone."

I nodded absently, then suddenly remembered something. "Hey, did I miss your birthday?"

"Yeah, two days ago. It was my best birthday ever."

The sarcasm was obvious in his voice. I frowned. "I'm sorry this is how you had to spend your eighteenth birthday."

"At least out here I have a cave to call home." Charlie stood and turned to walk away.

CHAPTER 15

I waited until Charlie was out of eyesight before I stood. I swayed slightly. Although I'd never been drunk, I imagined that might be what it felt like. I walked back to the cave entrance and sat on the ground facing the river, with my back leaning against the outer wall. My breath was shallow; my heart beat rapidly. Although I felt better, I couldn't believe how weak I was—and tired. Although I tried to fight it, I dozed off several times. When I'd wake up, I would feed the fires and return to my seat, dozing and watching and waiting for Charlie to return.

It was late in the day before Charlie got back. He slipped stealthily into the camp and was nearly on top of me before I knew he was there.

"Hey," I said, "where'd you learn to sneak up on people?"

He shrugged, dropped his rucksack to the ground and walked to the river's edge. The rucksack looked heavy and lumpy. "I had a lot of time on my hands the last few days, so I practiced stealth walking."

"You got pretty good at it."

Charlie nodded, as he stared off into the forest. He seemed lost in thought.

"What's in the bag?" I asked.

Charlie didn't move. He just stood there at the edge of the river, motionless.

"What's in the bag?" I asked, doing my best impersonation of Brad Pitt's character from the movie *Seven*.

"Um, what?" Charlie turned, stared blankly at me. "What'd you say?"

I pointed to the rucksack. "What's in the bag?"

"Oh...just more pears and some blackberries."

I reached in, grabbed a pear, bit into it. "It's good."

"Yeah." Charlie turned and walked into the cave. "I'm a bit tired, Abe. I think I'll call it a night. You want to take first watch?"

I swallowed a big chunk of pear and nodded. "Sure. I'll keep an eye on the fires."

Charlie stretched out on the cave floor and tucked what was left of my sleeping bag under his head. I couldn't imagine how tired he must've been. While I'd been sleeping for days, he'd been working hard. Tending the fires. Catching fish. Making sure we were safe. Keeping me alive...*keeping me alive*. I frowned. There was no way on earth I could ever repay Charlie for what he'd done. I owed him my life.

Before long, Charlie was snoring, and I was fighting to keep my eyes open. I got up several times to stoke the fires. The last time I fed the fires, I decided to walk to the river and splash cold water on my face. Although the riverbank was within the fires' glow, it was dark and lonely, and I could almost feel dozens of pairs of eyes on me. I dropped to my knees, keeping a careful eye on my surroundings. A chill reverberated up and down my spine as I scooped up water with my cupped hands and slapped myself in the face. When I stood, I caught a glimpse of the moon in the rustling water. It added to the eerie feel of the place, and I hurried back to the cave. I was gasping for air when I reached it and sank to the ground, exhausted.

"I've got to get my strength back," I said out loud.

"You will."

I jerked and turned to see Charlie sitting up. He rubbed his face. "It's my turn to watch. Why don't you get some sleep?"

I nodded, moved deeper into the cave and lay on the hard ground. Before I knew it, I was dead to the world and dreaming of better times.

* * *

When I woke up, the sun was just creeping over the trees and shining down on the clearing along the river. Charlie was sitting cross-legged on that same slab of rock from several days earlier when he'd been killing the ants, except this time he was motionless, staring out into the forest like he'd done the evening before. I stood cautiously and picked my way across the cave until I was standing beside him.

"What gives, partner?" I asked.

Charlie didn't look up. "We need to talk, Abe."

Curious, I sat on the rock beside him. "Shoot."

He paused for a long minute and finally said, "If you had a chance to get out of here, would you take it or would you stay?"

"What do you mean?"

"Would you go or would you stay?"

I looked around. "You mean, if I had the chance, would I leave this place and go back home?"

"That's exactly what I mean."

I grunted. "In a heartbeat."

"And you wouldn't consider staying?"

"No way. Why would I?"

"I figured you'd say that." Charlie sighed. "You have the world waiting for you, and I've got nothing."

"Come on, Charlie. Let's not rehash this. You've got a lot of things to look—"

"There's a cabin in the forest about ten miles that way." Charlie pointed downriver.

My mouth moved for several tries, but nothing came out. I swallowed hard and was finally able to get the words out. "Who lives there? Where are they?" I stood and looked around. "Are they getting help? What's going on? Why didn't they come back with you?"

"They don't know we're here," Charlie said.

"What do you mean?"

"I didn't make contact with them."

I sat down hard—harder than I'd wanted to because my weak legs gave out halfway down—and my mouth dropped open. "You didn't make contact with them. Why on earth not?"

Charlie shrugged. "I guess I wanted to talk to you first."

"To ask me if I wanted to be rescued?" I wished for my strength back so I could punch him in the face. "Of course I want to be rescued! This is not my idea of living. I want out of this godforsaken place and I don't ever want to come back—*ever!* What on earth would make you think otherwise?"

"I don't know. This place…it changes you. It makes you realize how simple life really is." Charlie stood and waved his arms around. "I mean, just look around you. We have the best view in the country. We have all the food we could hope for. We don't answer to anyone. Heck, we don't need anyone—or anything. The only rules are kill or be killed; eat others before they eat you. We took on the mountains and we won, like we took on the swamps and won. The bears aren't the king of the mountains anymore—we are. Out here, we rule. We don't answer to anyone. We're truly free."

Charlie paused and nodded; he seemed to stand taller. "I'm in control out here. All those punks who picked on me in school could never do what I did. They couldn't survive out here."

"Charlie, what's gotten into your head? You're talking crazy. We have a life back home. We can't just abandon everything to live out here like wild people. I want to take a shower. Brush my teeth. Eat a McDonald's hamburger. I want to box again. And what if we get hurt? What if my cuts get infected again? We're down to the bottom of the bottle of Tylenol, and we certainly can't make medicine. What if we get snake bit? Or fall off a cliff? That's not how I want to go out." I waved my hand to indicate the mountains around us. "And don't forget there's a killer out there just waiting to meet up with us again."

Charlie sighed and pursed his lips. "Fine. I'll hike out to the cabin again and get help for you, but I'm staying."

I threw up my hands. "That's ridiculous. You can't just move out here. First off, it's illegal. Second, you won't last very long."

Charlie stuck his chin out. "I've lasted this long, haven't I? I kept you alive for four days."

I'd never seen Charlie this sure or unreasonable about anything. At this point, I needed him and couldn't afford to piss him off. "You're right. You're right. You can make it out here on your own. You've proven that. Lord knows, I'd be dead if it hadn't been for you. Look, if you want to stay, there's nothing anyone can do about that, and I won't try to talk you out of it. I just need to get back home in time for orientation day."

Charlie stared deep into my eyes, as though trying to see right down to my soul. "So, you won't stay with me?"

"I'd love to Charlie, but my parents already paid for my first semester. And I've got plans for my life. I can't just shut them off and live an adventure. It sounds great, but I've got responsibilities now." I didn't want to tell him that this trip had forever cured me of my love for the outdoors. If I could just make it out of here alive I'd be happy to stare at high-rise buildings and drive along paved roads the rest of my life.

"Suit yourself." Charlie walked to the cave and grabbed his spear. "I'll make contact with the folks at the cabin and see what's what."

I studied Charlie's face. "What if I come along? I know I can make it if we take our time."

Charlie shook his head. "We'd never make it in one day with you stopping every few feet. It's at least ten miles over rough terrain and I'd have to carry you at places, and that would be too dangerous for both of us. Besides, if we'd get stuck out there in a storm we'd both be dead."

"I guess you're right." I didn't like it one bit, but there was no other way. I'd have to trust Charlie to bring back help.

"Don't worry," Charlie said. "I'll get you out of here and then I'll worry about myself."

I breathed a sigh of relief. "And I'll do whatever I can to help you get what you want when the time comes."

Charlie pulled on his shirt and took a couple of pears for the journey. "I'll be back sooner than you know."

I watched him walk away, and a sense of excitement started to burn inside me. We were finally going home. No more living in a cave. I'd be able to sleep in my bed again. Eat food with flavor, like shrimp stew and boiled crawfish. I'd get to drink Coke again. Go to college…*college.*

I suddenly remembered Joy. That sick feeling returned to my gut. My life was forever changed. What had happened to Joy was my fault, and I would never live it down. How on earth could I concentrate in college when I knew college was the reason I broke up with Joy? It was the reason she was probably dead out here somewhere in the mountains. Although I knew it was a waste, I said a silent prayer that she was hiding with her aunt.

I began to move about the cave, idly packing up everything in sight. I stuffed all of our meager supplies into my rucksack and then sat to take a breather. I began to shake, and I hoped I wasn't having a relapse of the fever. Sweat appeared on my forehead, and I wiped it away. I took several deep breaths. When my heart rate no longer sounded like a speed bag pounding against the inside of my chest, I continued cleaning up. I walked to the river and filled my bottle of water. Movement at the water's edge caught my eye. It was the rope. I tugged on it until the fish were in sight just under the surface. I thought about filleting and cooking them for our guests, but I didn't have a knife.

"Maybe we can take them with us," I said out loud, "and cook them at the cabin." I let the rope go, returned inside the cave, and looked around. There was nothing more to do except put out the fires, but I wasn't about to do that until Charlie returned with the posse. So I waited.

Throughout the day, dozens of deer walked along the opposite riverbank and a bear stalked the area around midday. He stopped to smell the spot where Charlie had stored the fish, he chewed the piece of fish meat I'd dropped on the ground earlier, and then he walked to the edge of the river and pawed at the rope that held Charlie's catch. It took him some time, but he finally pulled the fish to the rocks of the riverbank and started biting into them. I grabbed my spear and stepped cautiously out of the cave.

"Get out of here!" I stabbed the air with my spear as I yelled. "Go on! Leave that alone, you thief!" The bear turned his head, mouth agape, exposing two huge bottom teeth. He fixed me with his cold stare, and I just stood there frozen. He made a husky blowing sound and I regretted my decision to play the hero. I backed toward the depths of the cave, and he resumed his meal, realizing I was no challenge. When he was done, he ambled away, his large rump swaying back and forth as though waving his goodbye. I knelt on the ground, exhausted.

What seemed like a few more hours dragged by and still no sign of Charlie. The sun had already dipped behind the distant mountains to the west. Although I'd kept the fires burning bright, the area around me was cloaked in darkness. I tossed more wood on the fire and walked to the edge of its orange glow.

"Charlie!" I screamed as loud as I could. There was no response, except for my own voice echoing off the nearby mountains. I called his name for several minutes, stopping often to bend over and catch my breath. Lightheaded and weak, I crawled into the cave and assumed the fetal position next to the fire.

My mind began to wander and a recurring thought tried to creep its way into my reasoning, but I kept pushing it aside, trying to dismiss it as impossible. Instead, I focused on the possibility Charlie might have been attacked by a bear or hurt in some other way or... *Holy crap!* What if Leaf Creature had finally found us? What if it had killed Charlie and was backtracking him to the cave?

I began to tremble. If Charlie had been killed or taken, it would be up to me to get help. I wasn't sure exactly where he'd found the cabin, but I knew the general area and I might be able to track him. If I wanted to survive, I had to get to that cabin.

As the night dragged on and there was still no sign of Charlie, I began to consider all the possibilities—including the idea Charlie might have abandoned me. I shook my head to clear it. He would never do such a thing, no matter how bad he wanted to live out here. He would get help first and then disappear if that was what he intended. After all, I reasoned, if he wanted to abandon me, he would've done it by now, while I was sick and didn't know better.

*　　*　　*

At first light, I was on my feet. I made a dozen trips from the river to the fires, using my water bottle to douse the flames. When I was certain they were completely extinguished, I wolfed down two pears, drank a full bottle of water—even though I didn't feel I needed it—and slung my rucksack onto my shoulders. I stopped to catch my breath, then took one more look around the place I'd called home for the past week or so. With the spear dangling in my hand and the bow and two arrows tied onto my pack, I set off in the direction I'd last seen Charlie.

I followed the riverbank until I came to the clearing in the trees that marked the route to the meadows. I paused to catch my breath and wondered if I should continue following the river. Charlie had simply said it was ten miles "that way" and had pointed downriver, but that didn't mean he followed the river the entire time. Still unsure, I decided to follow the river. I counted my paces as I walked, using my spear as a crutch and stopping every half-mile to rest.

While I did feel stronger, this walk was zapping my energy reserves. I stopped at the three-mile mark and sat on a rock beside the river. I ate a pear and drank the entire bottle of water. I felt weak and seven miles seemed an impossible feat in my present condition. What would I do if I couldn't make it all the way? What if I couldn't find the cabin? Where would I sleep? What if I couldn't find proper shelter from the weather and animals? I suddenly felt vulnerable and alone.

I swear, if Charlie abandoned me on purpose, I will never—

A twig snapped somewhere downriver and to my right. I snatched up my spear and jumped to my feet, scanning the forest. There was no movement, no sound…nothing.

"Charlie? Is that you?" My voice surprised some nearby birds, and they darted away, their wings flapping a frightened tune on the wind. I held my breath and stood like a statue for several long minutes. A light breeze tickled the leaves—and my face—and I figured that must've been what made the noise. Satisfied there was nothing to worry about, I bent, picked up my water bottle, and refilled it in the river. I shoved it into the side pocket of my stained and matted cargo shorts and continued my trek along the riverbank.

I had paced off a hundred yards and was just walking by a patch of underbrush when I caught a flash of movement in my peripheral vision. It was behind me and to the right. I started to turn around, but something was shoved under my left armpit. It looped up in front of my left shoulder and hooked over the left side of my neck, forcing my head downward. Pain shot through the center of my spine. I started to yell, but a flash of white cloth slapped me full force in the face, cupping over my mouth and nose. I shot my right elbow backward with all the strength I could muster, but it landed on some sort of soft leafy cushion. I felt claustrophobic.

Panicked, I sucked inward and was surprised at how easy I was able to catch a breath. The air in that cloth was sweet. I took slow, deep breaths, trying to remain calm. I reached up with my right hand to grab at whatever it was that was holding the white cloth across my face. I grabbed a handful of leaves and twigs.

I'm being attacked by a giant bush!

Just as the realization struck me, my vision began to blur. My already weakened legs grew weaker. I felt dizzy. My body went limp, but I didn't fall. The powerful arms of the attacking bush held my sagging body upright. My last conscious thought was that my feet were dangling above the ground and it felt like I was being hoisted into the air.

CHAPTER 16

Soft hands caressed my face, and a soothing voice whispered in my ear. My head pounded. I eased my eyes open, allowing the light to shine through a little at a time. When my eyes were fully open, everything was cloudy, and I could only make out fuzzy shapes. I blinked several times, then reached up and rubbed them.

"It's okay. Take your time," the sweet voice said. "It'll take a few minutes to wear off. You'll feel a little nauseous for a while, but it'll pass."

The next time I opened my eyes, they were clear. I gasped. A girl was leaning over me. Her face was pale, her hair blood red. Although she was five years older now, there was no mistaking who she was. "Mable?" I asked. "Are you Mable Bragg?"

She jerked back. "How do you know my name?"

I started to sit up, but Mable gently pushed down on my chest.

"You need to rest," she said. "If you get up too fast, you could be sick."

"But where am I? Why are you here?" My mind raced like a crotch rocket zipping along the open highway. I looked past Mable at a shadow in the darkness of the enclosure. "Who's that?"

The girl came into view. I jerked to my feet and tried to rush to her, but my head spun, and I collapsed to the ground. She rushed to my side. "It's okay, Abraham. You need to rest."

My eyes were wide, and I was afraid they were deceiving me. "Joy! Where were you? Where are we? What happened? I thought you were dead!"

Joy placed a finger on my lips and looked at Mable. "I knew seeing me would upset him. I should've waited until he was stronger."

I shook my head. "I'm good. I promise. I'm just so glad to see you! I...oh God...I thought you were dead."

Tears flowed down Joy's face. "I didn't think I'd ever see you again—and that's what killed me the most!"

I couldn't contain my own emotions. I pulled Joy into my arms and shoved my face into her shoulder. As much as I hated to do so, I cried, too. "I'm so sorry, Joy. I was wrong. I shouldn't have broken up with you. It was so stupid of me. I do love you. I don't know—"

Joy pushed me back and pressed her lips to mine. I don't know how long we kissed, but it was the softest and most passionate kiss of my young life, and I didn't want it to end. When we stopped, I wiped the tears from my face with my hands so no one else would see.

"The important thing," Joy said, "is that you came for me. That tells me all I need to know about you."

"How do you know who I am?" Mable asked.

"There are signs—posters—by the trail we came in on. And Charlie found a news article online about all of y'all. Wait—where are the others? And where're Charlie and Brett?"

The girls just stared at each other. I pushed off the floor and sat up. The room spun a little, so I took a moment to gather myself and checked out my surroundings. Joy and Mable wore matching white T-shirts, men's jeans—cut off at the knees—and flip-flops. The clothes looked to be the same size, but they fit Joy much better. I turned my attention to the room. We were in some sort of prison cell in what appeared to be an underground cavern.

"Where are we?"

"Somewhere beneath the Blue Summit Mountains," Mable said.

Our prison cell was about twenty feet by thirty feet and was furnished with four cots, a small table, three chairs, and a sofa. Off to the back of the cell there was an area sectioned off with what looked like an oversized shower curtain.

Mable followed my gaze. "It's a bathroom—a sorry excuse for one, but a bathroom nonetheless."

The cavern was dimly lit by a number of lanterns that hung from pegs in the hallway outside the prison bars. Through the rustic bars, I could see the cavern opened up into a large storage area off to the right. Metal shelves lined the walls and the shelves were stocked from top to bottom with boxes upon boxes of goods. With Joy's help, I stood. I wrapped an arm around her shoulder until the room stopped spinning.

A narrow hallway separated our cell from another cell. I looked through the bars directly across the hall and realized it was a mirror image of our cell. There were two girls leaning over a figure lying on a military cot. I immediately recognized those cargo shorts. I stumbled to the bars, wincing as my head seemed to split in two. "Charlie! Charlie, are you okay?"

One of the girls looked up. It was Jillian Wagner. The other girl was Jennifer Banks. They were dressed identical to Joy and Mable. My head spun again. I grabbed the bars to keep from falling. "What's going on? How are y'all alive? Everyone thinks y'all are dead. What's wrong with Charlie?"

Mable appeared beside me. "Who thinks we're dead?"

"Everyone. The whole world. The park rangers say y'all committed some ritualistic suicide or something by going back to nature."

"Me, too?" Joy asked.

"They think you ran away or something because of the fight you had with your dad." I walked to our cell door and shook it as hard as I could. It rattled, but was held in place by a chain and padlock. The bars appeared to be something straight out of the Civil War era, but the chain and padlock were modern. I began to panic. "Charlie! Charlie, get up! We need to get out of here."

"There's no way out," Mable said.

I turned to face her. "What's wrong with Charlie? Will he be okay?"

Jillian, who had been missing the longest and should, by my estimation, be twenty-three years old, looked up from where she tended to Charlie. "He'll be fine. He must've been given a large dose. He'll start feeling better within a day or so."

"Large dose of what?" I asked.

Jillian shrugged. "Chloroform, most likely. The stuff's easy enough to make and everyone who comes in here says the mysterious white napkin that was cupped over their face smelled sweet."

"That happened to me, too." I didn't say anything about the bush because I didn't want to sound crazy.

I stared from one girl to the other. They all looked to be well fed and, for missing people, seemed in good spirits—except for Joy. It seemed the other girls had long ago accepted the fact they would be stuck down here for the rest of their lives. Joy had not.

I pursed my lips. "I've got to get out of here. They'll be looking for us, and if we're underground, they'll never find us."

"I know," Jillian called from her cell. "That's why he keeps us down here, so no one will ever find us."

"What about Brett? Was he brought here?"

Joy frowned. "That kid who transferred from Arkansas?"

I nodded.

"We haven't seen him." Joy said. "What's he doing out here?"

"He came with me and Charlie." They hadn't seen Brett, which meant he was probably dead. My blood ran cold. This wasn't a drill. This was the real deal. Charlie and I were trapped underground with four girls who were presumed dead. The finality and hopelessness of the situation settled like a bomb at the bottom of my stomach and exploded. I rushed to the bathroom. I tore back the curtain and dropped to my knees in front of a wooden bucket to vomit what little food I'd recently eaten. It was darker in the bathroom and I couldn't tell if I got any on the floor. I wiped my mouth on the front of my shirt and slowly stood.

"It happened to all of us," Mable said from outside the curtain.

I nodded and made my way back to the bars of our cell with Joy by my side. She grabbed my hand and squeezed tight. I had a million questions for her and the other girls, but didn't know where to start. I suddenly remembered the boys who'd gone missing and Katherine Turner. "What about Woody Lawson, Dave Burke, and Katherine Turner?" I looked through the bars. "Are they in another cell?"

Jillian shook her head. "They're gone."

"They escaped?" I asked. "How?"

Jillian shook her head slowly. "They're dead."

I frowned. "What happened to them?"

Charlie started moaning, turned to his side and heaved. Jillian grabbed a bucket while Jennifer guided Charlie's head toward it. He vomited for several seconds. I began to shake and gripped the bars harder to conceal my nervousness. "Will he be okay?"

Joy rubbed my shoulder. "He'll be fine. Jillian knows what she's doing. She told them how to take care of me."

When Charlie stopped vomiting and was lying comfortably on his back, I turned and walked to the sofa. It felt good to sit on something other than a hard rock. Joy jumped on the sofa to my left, Mable to my right.

"It's tradition," Mable said. "You have to tell us everything."

Puzzled, I rotated my gaze from Joy to Mable, who sat like an eager buzzard waiting for me to die, and then back to Joy. "What is she talking about?"

"We've been cut off from the world for a long time," Mable said.

"Some of us longer than others," Jillian called from the other cell.

"So," Mable continued, "the new person has to tell us what's been going on since we left."

Joy rolled her eyes. "They did it to me, too. I felt like I was being interrogated."

"Um, I…I don't know where to start." My thoughts raced. I had to find a way out of this place.

"Start by telling us about you," Jillian said. She sat facing our cell while she rubbed Charlie's forehead with a wet rag. "It helps to break the ice."

"That's really not necessary." Mable shot her thumb at Joy. "She already told us everything about you."

I glanced sideways at Joy. "What'd you tell them? That I was a fool and an ass?"

"No, I told them how great of a guy you are and how lucky I was to be your girlfriend."

That stung. I would've felt better had she trashed me.

Mable slapped the floor in front of her. "What's been happening out there? Any more terrorist attacks in the US? Killer hurricanes or tornadoes? What's the big news of the day?"

"This should be good." Joy folded her arms across her chest. "I can't wait to hear what you think is important in the world."

"Didn't you update them already?" I asked.

Joy nodded. "I gave them the important stuff. I'd love to hear things from your point of view."

"Um…a year ago Manny Pacquiao was robbed of his championship belts. It was one of the most—"

"Who's Manny Pac-cow?" Jennifer asked.

"Is he the guy who won *American Idol?*" Mable asked.

"*American Idol*…what? No." I scowled at their ignorance of the subject. "He's only the best boxer who ever lived."

"Boring," Jennifer said. "Tell us something else."

"The Saints won the Super Bowl a little over three years—"

"Dave already told us that," Mable said. "Tell us something we care about. Any good movies coming out? New bands? Cool line of clothes or shoes? Stuff like that."

I scratched my head and tried to focus my thoughts on what news they might be interested in. "Part two of *The Hunger Games* is coming out next year. All the girls liked the first one."

"Did you say *Hunger Games?*" Jillian asked.

"Yeah," I said absently. "It's about—"

"We know what it's about. It was the last book Katherine read before she was kidnapped. She told us all about it." Jillian was leaning against the bars of her cell. "So, they made the books into some movies, eh? That's wonderful. Who plays Katniss?"

"Um, who's Katniss?" I asked.

"The main character," Jillian said. "I thought you knew what it was about?"

"I never actually saw it," I admitted. "I heard the girls at school talking about it."

"You don't know who plays her?" Mable asked.

"I don't know her name, but I think it's the blue girl from the last *X-Men* movie," I said.

Mable clapped her hands. "Very good—that's close enough. But we already know who plays her. Like Joy said, she updated us on the important things."

The girls talked among themselves about movies they had seen and books they'd read. I sat back and watched in awe, wondering how they could be so calm in this situation. If I didn't know better, I'd think they were sitting in their living rooms passing the time. Their voices slowly faded to a dull drone as my thoughts raced. Why weren't they looking for a way out? Why weren't they planning an escape?

They didn't look in a hurry to go anywhere, and that scared the heck out of me. Would that be me in a year from now? Drained of hope? Accepting my plight and resigning myself to living underground for the rest of my life? I'd read somewhere about this Stockholm syndrome thingy and I wondered if they suffered from it—wondered if their kidnapper had somehow connected with them and they were now on his side. If so, they might stifle our attempts at escaping.

When there was a break in their conversation, I turned to Mable. "Who's responsible for this? Who kidnapped us?"

Mable shook her head. "We don't know."

"What's he look like?" I asked.

"We don't know," Mable said. "We've never seen his face."

I stared across the way at Jennifer and Jillian. "None of y'all?"

They all shook their heads. Jillian looked at Jennifer and then back to me. "The only thing we know for sure is that he dresses like a giant bush."

"A bush?" I squinted, thinking back. It finally connected. "The thing that attacked me was wearing some kind of leafy suit. It makes sense now."

"What does?" Mable asked.

"The suit allows him to get close to his victims without being detected, and it also helps him disappear." I nodded, impressed. "It worked like a charm. I walked right beside him when he grabbed me—never even saw him coming. The same thing happened with Brett."

Charlie moaned and sat up in his cot. Jillian helped hold him steady. He looked dazed. I turned to Mable. "What happened to Woody, Dave, and Katherine?"

"Woody died roughly two years ago," Mable said.

"How?" I asked.

"He drowned. It was a bad idea. He'd been saying he thought he could find a way out of here through that little pool of water. He said it had to go somewhere." Mable shook her head. "We tried to talk him out of it, but it was no use. He faked a seizure when Mr. Bush was bringing our food one day and—"

"Wait," I interrupted. "Y'all call this creature *Mr. Bush?*"

"Yeah," Mable said. "Is that a problem?"

I smiled. "We call him Leaf Creature."

Mable smiled back. "Mr. Bush opened the door to check on him. Woody caught him by surprise and pushed him down and made a run for it." Mable smiled, stared off into the distance. "I swear we could hear him giggle when he hit that water."

"He was going to be an Olympic swimmer," Jennifer said. "He was like a fish in the water."

Mable nodded. "He used to stare at that pool of water every day, like a sad little puppy staring at the back door just waiting for his owners to come outside and play with him."

"He figured that water was the only way out of here," Jillian said. "And he was right."

I looked around. "What water are y'all talking about?"

Joy took my hand and led me to the far right of our cell and pointed to the back wall of the cavern, where a small pool of water was positioned.

I gasped. "Where does it go?"

"We don't know," Mable said.

"He made it out of here?" I asked.

"Yeah, but not the way you think," Mable said.

"He reappeared five days later," Jillian said.

My brows puckered. "Reappeared?"

"His body floated to the surface five days after he jumped in," Jillian said. "He was face down and swollen."

"And he stunk something awful," Mable said. "Mr. Bush came down and took his body away that night."

I looked at the ceiling of the cavern. There was not even the slightest hint of light from the outside world. "How'd y'all know it was five days? I mean, how do you even keep track of time in here? Myself, I don't know if I've been here one day or three."

Joy grabbed my hand again—I was starting to think she was looking for excuses to hold it, and I didn't mind at all—and led me back to the door of our cell. She pointed toward Jillian's cell. "Jill, show him."

Jillian walked to the curtain at the back of their cell and pulled it back. Above the horse trough that served as a bathtub, small lines had been scratched into the rocky wall of the cave—seven rows of marks. "Mr. Bush feeds us twice every day. The first meal is small and the second one is big, and we make one mark for every big meal we get." Jillian pointed to the first mark on the first row. "I made that mark the very first day I was brought here." She turned around, and I thought I saw her eyes glistening. "It seems like a lifetime ago."

Jennifer walked over and hugged her.

Charlie was leaning on one elbow, swaying. "What's going on here?" His speech was slurred.

I moved to the bars of my cell. "How you feeling, buddy?"

He looked up, squinted. "Abe? What're you doing out of school?"

"I came looking for you and—"

Charlie lurched forward and vomited again. Jillian and Jennifer tended to him, and I turned away, not wanting to see my friend in that condition. As I squatted, I shook my head. "I should've come alone. I got Brett killed and look at Charlie. This was my cross to bear."

"You came out here to find Joy?" Jillian wanted to know.

"Yeah. Everyone else gave up the search." I stood and looked down at Joy. "I couldn't live with myself. I had to come out here and try to find you—to make it right."

"You said there was an article about us?" Mable asked.

I nodded, pointing first at Jillian and then at Jennifer. "According to the police, you're both dead—killed by your boyfriends."

There was a collective gasp from both girls.

"Are you serious?" Jillian asked.

I nodded.

"What about me?" Mable wanted to know.

I went down the list, reciting everything I could remember from the online article Charlie had saved. When I was done, I asked about Dave and Jennifer.

"Dave was the last one to get here," Mable said. "Well, before you guys showed up. He was some kind of ghost hunter." Mable shook her head. "Anyway, he fell ill. When Mr. Bush came down to feed us, we tried to tell him, but he wouldn't listen. I guess he thought Dave was trying to trick him like Woody had. He was having none of it. Dave's condition got worse and, about a week or so later, he died in his sleep."

"Did the bush believe y'all then?" I asked.

Mable nodded. "He waited a couple of days before taking the body out."

"How long ago did Dave die?" I asked.

"Recently—about three months ago." Mable frowned, and I thought I saw a tear break free from her left eye and slide down her cheek. "We found Katherine hanging in the bathroom about a week later. She liked Dave and didn't want to live without him."

I tried hard to control the panic creeping up into my throat, choking me. We could all die in this place, and no one would ever know what happened to us—just like Woody, Katherine, Dave, and Brett. My thoughts turned to my mom and dad. They would be out there handing out fliers, wondering what had happened, giving tearful press conferences. After a few weeks, we would be presumed dead, and they would return home. Dad would go back to work. Mom would go back to doing whatever it was she did when Dad was at work. The whole world would continue on, and we would eventually be forgotten by most and become a distant memory to those few who loved us.

I heard a loud clanking sound down the hallway to the left. Joy grabbed my arm. "That's *him*. It's supper time."

I walked to the far left of our cell and craned my neck to see through the bars. There were metal rungs bolted into the rock wall. They formed a ladder that disappeared upward into a hole in the ceiling. Old hinges squeaked from somewhere far above and a beam of light shot down from the hole in the ceiling. Heavy boots thudded against the rungs and echoed ominously through the cavern as our captor made his way down into our prison.

CHAPTER 17

I watched with bated breath as one boot came into view and then the next. When he had descended all the way to the floor of the cavern, he turned and looked in my direction. I gulped out loud. He looked like he'd stepped straight out of a horror film. If I'd seen this guy walking around the swamps of Louisiana I would've sworn the Swamp Thing was real. His entire body was wrapped in leaves and tree branches, except for his face and his hands. He wore camouflage gloves and his face was wrapped in camouflage burlap with three slits cut into it for his eyes and mouth. He held a bucket in his left hand, and I couldn't help but wonder if it was filled with human body parts.

He stepped toward my cell, and I instinctively backed away. I was angry at myself for being afraid. Joy and Mable huddled behind me, and Jillian and Jennifer cowered in a corner of their cell. Charlie was lying on his cot, moaning, oblivious to what was taking place.

When the bush reached our cell, he pulled out three flat containers with lids out of the bucket and slid them under a gap in the bars. He then turned to the other cell and slid their food containers under the gap in their bars. He walked back to the rungs in the wall, disappeared upstairs for a few minutes, and returned with six canteens slung over his shoulder. He placed three on each side, then disappeared for good, slamming the hatch door shut with a finality that made me shudder.

As soon as the hatch was shut, the girls moved to the containers and began pulling the tops off. Before taking a bite of their food, Jillian and Jennifer took a plate to Charlie, helped him sit up, and began feeding him. The smell of freshly cooked meat and gravy filled the cavern and made my stomach growl. Joy handed me a container and a fork, flashing her sweet smile. "I know he's a bad guy and he's scary, but he can really cook."

"He acts like we're dogs." I took the plate and examined the food. It looked like deer meat and gravy over rice and there were beans and a bread roll on the side. "How do we know he hasn't poisoned the food?"

"If so, we would've been dead years ago," Jillian called from her cell.

I nodded, took my seat with Joy and Mable, and tested the food on my plate. It was flavored to perfection, with just the right amount of salt. While I didn't want to admit it, Joy was right—this mountain creep really could cook. We ate in virtual silence, the only sounds being the chomping of our teeth and the clanking of our forks against the containers. I twisted the top off my canteen and took a cautious sip. Lemonade. I tossed it back and drank nearly half of it in the first gulp. I couldn't remember the last time I'd eaten this well.

After supper, I watched Jillian walk to the back of her cell and scratch another mark into the wall. "It's been almost seven years since I was abducted."

No one commented, so I kept my own mouth shut. Mable stood from the table and turned to me. "Slip the containers, canteens, and silverware back through the bars. He'll be back soon to take them away. If anything's missing, there'll be hell to pay."

I studied my fork longingly. It would make for a decent weapon, and I welcomed the chance for him to step in this cell with me, but I didn't want to bring trouble down on the girls, so I did as I was told. Our dishes were sitting out in the hallway for about twenty minutes before the hatch opened again and Mr. Bush reappeared to take away the containers, utensils, and canteens. Before he left for the night, he blew out all the lanterns except for the two closest to the rungs in the wall, leaving the cavern cloaked in near darkness.

"Does he follow this same pattern every day?" I asked from where I leaned against the bars, watching his shadow ascend the ladder to the hole in the ceiling of the cavern.

"For the most part," Jillian said. "It's hard to keep track of time in here, but a few times each year he's extremely late bringing us food, and each time he returns, he's either got supplies or he's kidnapped another person."

"Except for last year," Mable said. "He didn't bring anyone new."

Jillian nodded her head to Joy, Charlie, and then me. "This is the first time he's kidnapped three people so close together."

I grunted, cursing myself for allowing this to happen. I turned back to my cell, where Mable and Joy were getting ready for bed. Charlie was already sleeping soundly across the hall, and I could hear Jillian and Jennifer moving about. Joy had pushed her cot next to mine and was fluffing her pillow. She then stretched out on it and stared up at me.

I walked to her and slipped onto my cot, rolling on my shoulder so I could look at her. Her eyes were moist and her lips trembled. "I'm so scared, Abe."

I scooted closer to her, and she crawled up against me, resting her head against my chest. I knew if I wasn't careful, I'd forget where I was and start to think everything was okay. I lay there holding Joy, staring up at the dark ceiling. Although it wasn't as comfortable as my bed back home, this cot was much better than the unforgiving rocks Charlie and I'd been forced to sleep on during the past week or so. I flexed my right fist, testing the pain in my forearm. Other than a dull pinch, it was healing up nicely.

"What happened to your arm?" Joy rubbed the bandage. "I noticed it when he first brought you in here."

"A bear attacked me."

Even in the shadows, I could see her eyes widen. "Are you serious?"

"Luckily, he only wanted the food behind me. If he'd wanted to kill me, there's not much I could've done except bleed." I leaned up on my elbow and looked over toward the other cot. "Mable, why do you think this guy kidnapped y'all? I mean, what does he do with y'all beside feed y'all?"

"Nothing, really."

"Then why would he just stuff y'all underground for all these years? Why keep y'all alive? What's he up to?"

Mable was silent for almost a minute. "I really don't know. We've talked about that a lot over the years. Jillian thinks he might be saving us to harvest our organs for himself or to sell on the black market."

"Hmm, that's a thought." I pondered this theory for a few minutes, but then dismissed it. "That can't be it. There'd have to be blood tests to see if y'all match him or his clients—and that would come before the abduction; otherwise, he could kidnap thousands of people before finding the right one, and that would be a lot of wasted time and effort."

"But then why?" Joy asked. "What does he want with us?"

"Has he ever hurt any of y'all?"

"No."

I paused, trying to decide how to frame my next question. My heart pounded in my chest as I thought about him doing anything to Joy. "Has he done anything bad...you know, *really* bad...to y'all?"

"He's never touched any of us," Mable said. "He's never even said a word to any of us. We've tried talking to him at times to ask why he was doing this to us, but he's never said a word."

"You've never heard his voice?" I asked. "Ever?"

"The only sound that ever came out of his mouth was when Woody escaped, and he didn't really talk. It was more like a growl—an angry growl. Like a mad dog." Mable shuddered. "He was so mad. I thought he was going to kill us all. He grabbed some of his shelves and pulled them down, started throwing his supplies around. He looked and sounded like an animal."

"Maybe he can't talk," I said.

"We thought of that. We also thought he might be part human and part animal."

I laughed.

"I'm serious," Mable said, sounding offended.

"I'm sorry," I said quickly. "I thought you said you thought he was part human and part animal."

"I did say that."

I lay back down, pulled Joy closer. "I don't think you have to worry about that."

"How can you be so sure?" Mable asked.

"Trust me...he's human." I then changed the subject and asked Joy how she had been abducted.

"My dad and I had gotten into a fight, and I stormed off, thinking I'd walk to the car on my own. I walked for about an hour and when I didn't see anyone, I got scared. I had this feeling like someone was watching me and—"

"I had that same feeling!"

"It was really scary. I decided to go back and find my parents. I was just walking along the trail and suddenly something came out of the bushes and grabbed me." Joy shuddered. "That was the scariest moment of my life. And that's all I remember."

We spoke softly for about an hour—trying not to wake the others—and somewhere along the way she drifted off to sleep, her last sentence an unintelligible gurgle about some cat named Sparky. I closed my own eyes, but couldn't go to sleep right away. I shivered, so I reached for a nearby blanket. Although it was the middle of summer, it was cold in these mountains, and I found myself craving the blistering heat of the Louisiana sun. Had I been told a month ago I'd miss being home once I was gone, I would've vehemently denied it, but here I was as miserable and homesick as that dog my mom used to talk about—she was called Lassie or something.

As I lay there, I began to consider our escape options. If I was going to get Joy and the other girls out of here alive, Charlie and I would have to do something—and do it soon. Somewhere in the darkness of the cavern I thought I heard gentle crying. Mable and Joy were breathing steadily beside me, so I knew it wasn't them. It had to be either Jennifer or Jillian. While I felt bad for them, it was good to hear them crying—it meant they wanted to leave this place as much as I did.

*   *   *

I was awakened by the sound of voices and the smell of bacon. I stirred in my cot, then pushed myself to a sitting position. Joy and Mable were placing the food containers on the table. Joy looked over. "Hey, sleepy-head, I thought you'd never wake up."

I rubbed my face. "I can't remember the last time I slept that good." I turned to see what Charlie was up to. He was sitting at the other table with Jennifer and Jillian. I walked to the bars. "How you feeling, Charlie?"

He looked up, his cheeks puffed out from the food in his mouth. He chewed quickly, swallowed. "Other than being a prisoner at the center of the earth and having a massive headache, I feel good."

"What happened to you?" I asked. "You were supposed to go get help at that cabin, but you never came back."

"I could ask you the same thing," he said. "If there's anybody in the world that's un-abductable, I would've guessed it was you. How'd he get the drop on you?"

"He just came out of nowhere." I shook my head. "I tried to fight back, but I couldn't. I was still too weak. What about you?"

Charlie took his plate of food and carried it with him to the bars of his cell, eating as he talked. "Well, I made it to the cabin."

I cocked my head sideways. "You did?"

"Yeah, that's where I was taken. When I got to it, I banged on the door, but nobody answered. The door was unlocked, so I went inside and looked around. I found some fresh-baked bread on the stovetop and took a piece while I searched inside the cabin. I called out a bunch of times, but nobody answered.

"I saw one of those tree suits hanging against the wall. When I walked by it, it dropped on top of me and put a white handkerchief across my face. I fought hard, but he held that rag against my face. I finally passed out. That's the last thing I remember until I woke up in here this morning."

"You don't remember vomiting last night? Or being spoonfed your supper?" I asked.

Charlie paused, a piece of bacon hanging from his mouth. "Who spoonfed me?"

"We did," Jennifer and Jillian said.

Charlie beamed as he nodded his head in approval. "I could get used to this."

"Before you get too excited," I said, "you should know you vomited all over them."

Charlie spat his food out of his mouth. He turned to look at Jillian and Jennifer, who sat at the table eating. "Did I really?"

They smiled and nodded. "But it's okay," Jillian said. "We've all been through it, and we all reacted the same way when we came down off the medicine."

"Jillian, who took care of you?" I asked.

"Mr. Bush," Jillian said.

"You were all alone with him?" Charlie asked.

Jillian nodded. "For about a year—until Woody got here. It was really scary."

I walked to our table and wolfed my breakfast down next to Joy and Mable. After we were done and Mr. Bush had retrieved our dishes and locked us inside the cavern again, I called everyone to huddle near the bars. "We need to try and figure a way out of here," I said.

"There's no way out," Jennifer said.

"Well, we'll have to see about that." I turned to Jillian. "Has he ever given any indication why he kidnaps people and brings them here?"

Jillian shook her head.

"We're breeding stock," Charlie said simply.

We all looked at him, a quizzical expression on all of our faces. "What are you talking about?" Jillian asked.

"While I was digging around the cabin, I found some interesting paperwork." Charlie looked over at me. "A lot of articles about the world coming to an end and a lot of manuals on surviving a nuclear explosion and other types of widespread disasters. There was also a Mayan calendar hanging in one of the rooms."

"What does any of that have to do with being breeding stock?" I asked.

Mable looked at me. "What's he mean by breeding stock?"

"I found a notebook with a lot of handwritten stuff in it," Charlie said. "While his handwriting is hard to read, I found where he had a plan to survive underground for three years, beginning December of 2012. Apparently, whatever was supposed to happen was supposed to happen back then and he was stockpiling enough food, water, and supplies for six people—him and five others."

"Don't you mean six others?" I asked.

Charlie shook his head. "He had plans for four girls, one boy, and him."

"Oh," I said. "Dave must've been a replacement for Woody."

"I don't get it," Mable said. "Why would he need to replace Woody?"

"Oh, crap, I get it," Jillian said. "He needed a guy to go along with us so he can repopulate the earth. He was going to start breeding us once the human race up there"—Jillian pointed to the cavern ceiling—"was annihilated."

There was a collective gasp among the other girls.

"Wait a minute," Jillian said. "If he had a Mayan calendar, that must mean he thought the world would end in December 2012."

"Your point?" Charlie asked.

"December of 2012 was eight months ago and nothing happened—so why are we still here?" Jillian asked. "Why hasn't he released us? And why did he kidnap you two?"

"That last one's easy," I said. "He took us to protect his secret. We caught him kidnapping Brett."

"Maybe there's a new date," Mable offered. "Maybe they pushed it back a couple of years? You know how some preachers say Jesus is coming back on a certain day? Then when that day comes and Jesus doesn't show up, they move the date."

"Well, I'm not waiting around to find out," I said. "I'm getting out of here, and I'm getting out soon."

"There's no way out," Jillian said.

"If a swimmer can get out of this cell, I can, too." I walked along the bars, pulling on each of them individually, testing them for signs of weakness. When I reached the far left end of our cell, I started walking back, scanning the bars of Charlie's cell. I walked until I was directly across from Charlie and then froze in place, pointing excitedly at Charlie's feet. "Your shoes! The safety pins on your shoes. You know how to pick locks, you little thief! You can open the doors."

CHAPTER 18

The girls and I kept watch while Charlie prepared to work on the padlock to his cell. He had removed two of the bigger safety pins from his shoes and bent one into a hook. "Jillian, can you hold the lock steady for me?" he asked.

Jillian quickly moved beside him and held the padlock in place while he manipulated the tumblers with one of the pins and held tension on the keyhole with the other, ready to turn it when the tumblers all fell into place.

I looked up to scan the ceiling of the cavern. "I sure hope he doesn't have hidden cameras in here."

Without looking up, Charlie scoffed. "We're in the middle of the mountains, my young friend. We don't even have lights or running water up here."

I flashed a sheepish smile. "I forgot where we were for a minute."

Mable nodded her understanding. "That happens to all of us. I remember one time we were talking and Jennifer asked what was playing on TV."

"I've got it." Charlie twisted the padlock and pulled it free. He tossed it aside and slowly opened the cell door. It creaked angrily, and Charlie paused—mouth half open—listening for any sound of movement above us.

"You're good," I said.

Charlie nodded, pushed the cell door some more and then stepped out. Jillian and Jennifer stared wide-eyed at the opening, afraid to walk through the door. Charlie looked back at them and nodded. "It's okay. Y'all can come out."

Tears welled up in Jillian's eyes as she took one careful step after another until she was standing in the hallway. "This is the first time in seven years I've been out of my cell."

Jennifer wrapped her arms around Jillian, and Jillian broke down. "It's okay, Jill," Jennifer said. "Let it all out. You deserve it."

"Yeah," Mable said. "You deserve to let it all out. You're the one who held us together for all these years. Now it's our turn to hold you together."

Charlie hurried to my cell door, dropped to his knees, and worked on the padlock. I held it steady for him. "What's the plan when you get it open?" I asked.

"This was your idea," Charlie said. "I thought you had everything figured out."

I glanced toward the rungs on the cavern wall. "Maybe we can ambush him the next time he comes down to feed us."

Charlie looked up at me. "Are you feeling stronger?"

I nodded. "I'll take him out this time. The element of surprise will be on my side."

The padlock wriggled in my hand as Charlie worked on the tumblers with one of the safety pins. He would occasionally try to rotate the keyhole with the other safety pin, but it was giving him fits.

"What's wrong?" I asked.

"This one's a little harder to get," Charlie said. "The tumblers feel a little—"

"He's coming," Jennifer screamed. "He's coming!"

A yelp ripped from Jillian's throat as she rushed back into the cell, followed closely by Jennifer. Charlie worked feverishly on the lock. My eyes were glued to the rungs in the wall. I heard the creaking of the hatch and saw the beam of light shoot down through the opening.

"You have to hurry, Charlie," I said, looking down at his progress.

"I'm trying." Charlie's breathing quickened. The safety pin stabbed in and out of the keyhole. Heavy boots thudded on the rungs.

"Get back in your cell," I hissed. "Put your padlock back on."

"No, I can do this." Sweat poured from Charlie's forehead, dripping in his eyes. He blinked quickly. Rubbed his eyes against his shoulder. "I've got this."

My heart raced. Mr. Bush's legs appeared through the opening. "You don't have time, Charlie. Get back in your cell. *Now!*"

Charlie stole a quick glance toward the opening to the hatch. I followed his gaze. Mr. Bush's foot was about to touch the cavern floor. A flash of movement brought my attention back down to my cell door. Charlie was gone. The only evidence he had been there were the two safety pins protruding from the keyhole of my padlock. I looked around. Before I could scream my objection, Charlie went airborne and dove headlong into the pool of water.

Mr. Bush turned quickly when he heard the splash of water and rushed toward the pool. I snatched the safety pins from the padlock and slipped them into my pocket before running toward the far right side of my cell. Mr. Bush was pacing like a panther. He growled as he stared into the water. I counted the seconds in my head. They turned into minutes. Panic began to constrict my throat when I counted out four minutes in my head and there was no sign of Charlie. That was his limit. He would have to resurface soon for air and if he were to have a chance at escaping through the hatch, I would have to buy him some time and distract Mr. Bush.

"Hey, you freak!" I hollered. "Why don't you come here and face me like a man? Open this cell and I'll beat your face in. Come on, you big coward! Get in here!"

Mr. Bush didn't even acknowledge my existence as he moved from one side of the pool to the other, scanning the water. I ran over and grabbed one of the wooden chairs in my cell, picked it up, and smashed it to the ground. I grabbed a piece of chair leg and ran toward the cell. Using my forward momentum, I launched the chair leg through the bars. The wooden projectile hit Mr. Bush in the back of his head with a thump. He grunted as his head lurched forward. He turned and produced a silver revolver from somewhere inside his leafy suit. Pointing it at me, he ran toward my cell bars screaming.

I rushed backward, my eyes wide. I stumbled and fell back, landing hard on the ground. Shaking, I stared up at Mr. Bush. His hand shook as badly as I did, but for a much different reason. His gloved index finger was wrapped around the trigger, and I just knew it was about to go off. I'd heard that your life flashes before your eyes right before you die, but all I saw was an evil monster growling down at me.

Just when I thought the gun was about to go off, water splashed in the pool. We all turned to see Charlie flailing about, gasping for air. He treaded water and looked about, trying to get his bearings. He took in the situation. His eyes locked with mine, and he gave a solemn nod. "Abe, I'm going for it—five minutes!"

I jumped to my feet and bounced up and down. "Get under water," I screamed. "He's got a gun! Get under water!"

Charlie arched his back, took a final giant breath, and

disappeared beneath the surface of the water. Mr. Bush spun around and let out a blood-curdling cry. He shoved his gun toward the pool of water and pulled the trigger. The noise was deafening, piercing my eardrums. Shards of rock ricocheted into the air as the bullet splattered against the far cavern wall. Four more gunshots followed in quick succession and the bullets zipped into the water, sending droplets exploding into the air. My heart sank to my water shoes. I dropped to my knees, breathing a desperate prayer for Charlie's safety. Mr. Bush returned to the pool and stalked the water's edge, keeping his gun leveled on the spot where he last saw Charlie.

Joy moved beside me and grabbed my hand. I glanced around. Jennifer and Jillian were clinging to the bars of their cell, staring at the water with worry in their eyes. Mable was doing the same on our side. My mind's clock told me five minutes had come and gone. There was no sign of Charlie. He had surpassed his limit. I strained to see if I could detect even the tiniest of bubbles. Nothing. After another five minutes had passed and there was still no sign of Charlie, the evil Bush let out a malevolent giggle and stomped to Jillian's cell and returned the padlock to the chain. Before he walked away, something caught his eye next to the pool. He walked back toward the water and bent to pick up the object from the ground. It was Charlie's water shoe.

Although those safety pins had saved our butts a couple of times during this trip, I now wished Charlie had purchased new shoes. Had he done that, he'd be safely in his cell right then. Another thought occurred to me, and my heart sank. It had been my idea to pick the lock, so it was my fault he was gone. As I stared at the water, hoping Charlie had somehow found a way to set a new world record, his life began flashing before my eyes. Everything he'd told me about his early childhood, every minute we'd spent together, every funny thing he'd ever—

I jumped when loud screams interrupted my thoughts. I turned to see the girls hanging on the bars of the cells, yelling at Mr. Bush as he walked by. Jillian picked up a chair and threw it at the bars. He ignored them and disappeared up the ladder, then slammed the hatch shut. I turned absently and stumbled to the far right side of my cell. I sank to my knees and stared at the water, trying to wish Charlie to the surface.

Joy sat beside me and wrapped an arm around my shoulder. "He did a brave thing. He died trying to—"

"Don't say that!" I shrugged Joy's arm off and stood. I felt a lump in my throat and my eyes moistened a bit. Not wanting the girls to see me cry, I walked away, went into the bathroom area, pulled the curtain shut. I sat on the wooden bucket and buried my face in my shirt. My jaw burned. Tears threatened to pour. My body shook as I fought to control my emotions. I felt like a complete and utter loser. I'd gotten Brett killed and now Charlie—whose life would I ruin next?

*   *   *

It had probably been an hour since Charlie had disappeared in the pool of water, but it seemed like a week. Anger had replaced my sorrow, and I began to seethe. I gritted my teeth. Clenched my fists. Somehow, I had to make that crazy Bush pay for what he did. I would find a way.

I dug the safety pins from my pocket and knelt in front of my cell door. I fumbled with the padlock, trying to unlock it. If I was going to get revenge, I'd have to get out of here, but it proved to be no easy task. I cursed myself for not paying closer attention to how Charlie opened the first padlock. Joy had steered clear of me and hadn't spoken to me since I ran into the bathroom. She huddled by the far left corner of the cell with Mable, where they chatted with Jillian and Jennifer through the bars, watching me from a distance.

When I heard something, I stopped and turned to Joy. "What was that?"

They had quit talking and were staring wide-eyed. "I…I don't know," Joy said.

It had sounded like a muffled thump from somewhere above us. I put the safety pins away and leapt to my feet. Thinking quickly, I snatched up one of the legs from the chair I'd broken earlier and walked to where they sat. I shoved the chair leg through the bars and waited, my arm poised to throw it toward the rungs.

"What're you going to do?" Mable asked.

"If I can throw it hard enough at the back of his neck I might be able to paralyze him, or at least knock him unconscious," I said. "That way, once I get the padlock open, we can make our escape with no resistance."

Mable chewed her fingernails as that familiar square beam of light shot downward followed by the heavy thumps of boots descending the iron ladder. When the first boot came into view I cocked the chair leg back and held my breath. The next boot came down and I caught my breath. "What the…"

I dropped the stick when the feet below those skinny pale legs hit the cavern floor, and Charlie turned toward us, holding a giant axe in his hands.

"Oh my God, Charlie!" I was overcome with joy. A few rebel tears flowed down my cheeks. "What happened? How is this possible?"

"We don't have much time. Stand back." Charlie ran toward my cell door, lifted the axe high into the air, and brought it down hard on the padlock. I heard a pop, but it was still attached. Charlie gave it a second chop and the padlock snapped open. As Charlie turned toward the other cell door, I wriggled the padlock free and pushed the door open. I stood back to let Mable and Joy scurry through first. Charlie was able to pop the other padlock off in one shot, and Jillian and Jennifer ran out of the cell. They huddled in the hallway with Joy and Mable.

I slapped Charlie's back. "Good to see you again!"

He smiled big and tossed the axe aside. "My new record's seven-and-a-half minutes."

I whistled, as I looked toward the rungs. "What do we do next?"

"Get out of here before Mountzilla comes back."

Charlie led the way up the ladder, and I put a hand on each of the girls' back as they followed gingerly behind him. When they were all safely upstairs, I scampered up the rungs and found myself in a dank storage room. Charlie put a finger to his lips, easing the door open to peek through the crack. When he was sure all was clear, he waved us on. "This way."

We followed Charlie through several rooms of a log cabin and out onto a large wooden porch. I gasped when I saw the view from the deck. This cabin was at the top of a mountain ridge, and we could see for miles in three directions. Clouds were rolling in, and they looked angry. Charlie kept the lead as we walked down a series of shaky wooden steps and set off into the dense forest.

"Where're we going?" I asked, ducking a branch here, dodging a bush there.

"As far away from this place as we can go," Charlie said. "That freak is only a mile or two back there."

"What's he doing?" I asked.

"Looking for me," Charlie called over his shoulder, as he scrambled up the side of a hill. "That pool of water came out under a waterfall. I hid in the forest...doubled back to the cabin...when he came snooping around. I guess he figured I drowned...he had a long pole with a hook at the end...he was shoving it around in the water." Charlie stopped at the peak of the mountain, and we all caught up to him. He looked around. "What do you think, Abe?"

I scanned the area carefully, searching for any sign of life.

Nothing. I strained to penetrate the shadows of the forest, and I stared at it for a full minute before I realized what I was seeing. I pointed. "There—a trail."

"It looks like we made it out okay." Charlie turned from where he had been studying our escape route.

I held Joy's hand and helped her down the mountain. We all gathered together at the center of the trail, and the girls stared in awe at their surroundings. Jillian dropped to the ground and kissed it. "We're free," she whispered. "We're actually free."

Jennifer wept and threw her arms around Charlie. "Thank you so much for coming back for us."

"Yeah," Jillian said. "It's a very brave thing you did. You could've kept going and sent help, but you actually came back for us."

Charlie shook his head. "I didn't go back for y'all. I went back for my shoe."

We laughed. I pointed to the boots. "Where'd you get those?"

"They were in the cabin," Charlie said. He looked around. "We'd better keep going, or we won't be free for long."

I nodded. "Left or right?"

Charlie pointed left. "That'll take us far away from the cabin, so I think we should go that way."

The girls all nodded. "Sounds good to me," Jillian said. "The more distance we put between us and that cabin, the happier I'll be."

Charlie took the lead again, and I took rear guard. The day was going, and we needed to get as many miles under our feet as possible. The trail dipped and turned, hugging the mountains on one side and dropping precariously on the other. When we had traveled about eleven miles, we came upon a small stream that flowed alongside the trail. We took turns dropping to our knees and drinking some of the ice-cold water, the girls going first. When we were done, we split up and scouted the area, Mable and Joy coming with me and Jennifer and Jillian going with Charlie. The shadows were getting longer as dusk was setting in.

"Under no circumstances do any of you go off alone," I warned before we split up. They all nodded, and my group set off to the right of the trail, crossing the stream, and Charlie and his group set off to the left side of the trail. We had walked a hundred yards when we came across a section of rocky bluffs that extended skyward about twenty feet and angled slightly outward over our heads. I nodded. "This'll be perfect. If it rains we'll be covered."

I turned away and led Mable and Joy back toward the stream,

where we met up with Charlie, Jennifer, and Jillian.

"Remember those briars we fought with on that cliff?" Charlie asked.

I nodded.

"That's all we found on that side," Charlie said.

"That's okay," I said. "We found the perfect spot. It'll offer shelter from the rain and the ground cover is all rock, so we won't leave any shoeprints." I set off toward the bluffs, and everyone followed. When we reached it, we spread out and examined the area more closely. "We'll sleep three at a time," I said. "The other three of us will keep watch."

Jillian nodded. "That sounds like a good idea."

I pointed to Mable and Joy. "We'll take first watch."

Charlie, Jennifer, and Jillian found comfortable spots close to the base of the bluffs and curled up for the night. As a light drizzle began to fall out in the forest, Mable, Joy, and I sat side-by-side under the rocky overhang and stared out into the darkness. We made small talk in order to stay awake. When I figured half the night had gone by, I shook Charlie and all awake and we traded places. I curled up on the hard ground—with Joy pressed against me—and was asleep almost as soon as my head hit my rocky pillow.

CHAPTER 19

My eyes shot open and I sat upright. It was daylight, and the girls were scattered around the base of the bluffs, sound asleep. Charlie was propped against a large boulder, his head tilted back and his mouth open. Something had stirred me from my sleep. I scanned my surroundings. Nothing appeared out of the ordinary. Everything was quiet. Except—

I jumped to my feet as a strong breeze carried the distinct and rapid "whop-whop-whop" sound of helicopter blades.

"Get up! We're being rescued!"

Not waiting to see if anyone had heeded my cries, I broke out running across the rocky ground toward the stream. Once I reached it, I plunged right into the water, high-stepping it down the stream, searching overhead for a gap in the treetops that was large enough to be seen from above. The helicopter drew nearer, the chopping of the blades louder. Just ahead, the stream bent to the right and I saw a clearing on the opposite bank. I raced for it, but just before I reached it, the helicopter zoomed by overhead. I hollered as loud as I could and jumped up and down like a fool, waving my arms in the air. The helicopter didn't slow down and didn't change course. It faded off into the distant sky, disappearing over the mountain ridges ahead of me.

I dropped to my knees in the freezing water, exhausted. That was the most I'd exerted myself since recovering from my infection...I was gassed. I cupped my hands in the stream and splashed water on my face. The cold liquid shocked me alert and I pulled myself to a standing position. *What if the helicopter reports to headquarters that this area is all clear?* No one would come back out here to look for us. *What if it isn't even a rescue helicopter, but some sightseeing bird out touring the Blue Summit Mountains?*

"Did you get them? Did they see you?"

I turned to see Charlie standing at the edge of the stream—palms planted against his knees—panting.

I shook my head. "They got away."

A few minutes later, twigs snapped and leaves rustled as the girls appeared at the river's edge, their eyebrows raised.

"Are we being rescued?" Jillian asked. I detected a subtle hint of restrained excitement in her voice.

It killed me to tell her the truth. "I'm so sorry, but I couldn't get its attention."

There was a collective sigh as the girls collapsed to the ground. Jillian lay on her back and placed her arm over her face. "I'm hungry, I stink, and I'm tired."

There was a chorus of agreement from the others. "I think I'd rather be back in prison," Jennifer said. "At least we were safe and had food to eat."

"Don't say that," Mable said. "We'll be okay. Abe and Charlie will get us home."

"How?" Jennifer asked. "We don't even know what direction we're supposed to go. We could die out here and be eaten by wild animals and never found. We should've never left the cave."

Mable crossed her arms, her jaw set. "They got us this far and they'll get us home."

Jillian moved her arm away from her face and stared over at Jennifer. "As for me, I'd rather die out here in the wilderness a free woman than live one more day as a prisoner in that cave."

"Nobody's dying," I said, trying to sound more confident than I felt. I stood and trudged out of the stream. "Let's keep moving. This trail has to lead somewhere."

After we all took turns drinking from the icy stream, I led the way along the trail. We stopped often for me to catch my breath and for the girls to rest their feet. The flip-flops were less than ideal hiking shoes and they stumbled often along the way. Joy kept pace with me at the front of the line and we spoke as we navigated the narrow trail. I kept my eyes peeled for anything edible, but other than a couple of black bears, a squirrel, and a dozen deer, I saw nothing that would constitute food.

Jennifer complained often about being hungry and, although I kept my own complaints to myself, I felt her pain. My energy had been depleted long ago and I was working off pure will to live. I knew Mr. Bush would not give up and he was probably out there stalking us and waiting for his chance to recapture us all, one at a time. We knew where his cabin was located, and that made us a liability. I didn't know how far he would go to protect his secret, but I imagined he would resort to killing if he had to.

*   *   *

It had to have been getting close to seven or eight o'clock when Charlie walked to the front of the line and waved me to a stop. His face was gaunt and there were bags under his eyes. "It looks like this trail has doubled back toward where we came."

I looked up at what was left of the sun. He was right. "What're you thinking?"

"Maybe it's taking us deeper into the backcountry, away from civilization."

"We're going deeper into the wilderness?" Jennifer asked.

"We need to find a place to bed down for the night," I said.

Jennifer tugged at my arm. "Well? Are we?"

I shrugged. "I'm not sure."

We hadn't seen any more helicopters, so that led me to believe the one from earlier was random and not a part of any search party. I stared off into the dense forest. The shadows were starting to stretch and the light was growing dimmer.

"Did you see any blackberry bushes?" I asked.

Charlie's brows furrowed. "You think I saw them and just kept my mouth shut, preferring to slowly starve to death instead?"

"I guess you're right." My head ached. We had to eat. Remembering something I'd seen Charlie do, I walked off trail and began kicking rotten logs apart. I bent and plucked thick grubs from where they nestled in little dugouts in the logs. When I'd collected two handfuls, I rejoined the rest of my group on the trail.

"What're those for?" Katherine asked.

"That's dinner," Charlie said.

Jennifer made a face, but Jillian stepped forward. "I'll eat your left arm if you let me." She grabbed a couple of the grubs and shoved them into her mouth. After pinching her nose, she chewed and swallowed, scrunching her face as she did so.

The other girls watched wide-eyed.

"How was it?" Mable asked.

After smacking the taste away and wiping tears from her eyes, Jillian nodded. "Good. It tastes like chicken."

Joy went next and ate them without pinching her nose. I nodded my approval and held my hands out to Jennifer. She picked up one of the grubs. As she was bringing it to her mouth, it wriggled in her hand, and she shrieked and threw it across the ground. She shook her head. "I can't do this. I'd rather die of starvation."

"You need to eat something," I said. "Or your body will shut down."

She shook her head. "I won't do it."

"Suit yourself." I split the rest among Joy, Jillian, Mable, Charlie, and me. After we'd eaten them all, we spread out and began breaking up more logs, searching for more grubs to eat. Jennifer watched in disgust as we devoured everything we could find in the immediate area. I could only imagine how ridiculous we looked from her vantage point, scrambling around on our hands and knees, chasing these little wood-eating worms, but we didn't know when our next meal would be or from where it would come. Besides, they were small and it would take a lot of them even to begin to knock the sting off our hunger pangs.

"You really need to eat something," I told Jennifer, as I located another grub.

"I'd rather starve than eat that stuff." Jennifer turned. "I don't know how—"

The scream that ripped from Jennifer was so sudden and piercing that I nearly dove headlong into the large tree in front of me. I spun around and sucked in my breath. There on the trail, big as life, were two park rangers—a male and a female. The female park ranger's jaw seemed to sag down to her chest. "I...this...this can't be real. Dan"—she reached out and touched her partner's arm—"it's...it's them. We've looked everywhere for them." She pointed her finger at Jillian first and then counted the girls off one at a time, shaking her head in disbelief. "You're all here, except for Katherine, Woody, Dave and Brett. I don't understand it. How'd y'all all get to be together?"

Charlie stepped forward. "I found them underneath a cabin in the mountains. They were being held in an underground cave and were going to be used as breeding stock."

The female park ranger—whose nametag read Isabel Conner—turned to Charlie. "Rangers found Brett's body several days ago, but we've been looking for you and your friend for over a week now. How did you end up with them? Where're the other two boys?"

What followed was a blur of excited conversation, with everyone trying to talk at once. Isabel and Dan asked a million questions, and we all stepped on each other's words trying to answer them. When we mentioned Mr. Bush, it appeared to make Isabel uneasy, and I saw her hand drift to her sidearm and she began keeping a wary eye around the forest.

After about ten minutes of nonstop verbal fencing, things finally quieted down a bit, and Jennifer pointed to the rucksack on Dan's back and asked, "Do you have any food in there? They've all just finished eating supper, but I didn't get any."

"Absolutely," said Dan. He dropped his pack and dug in an outside pocket, then pulled out a handful of energy bars. He handed them out to us. "Eat these. It'll hold you over until we get to the shelter."

We ripped the paper from the energy bars and wolfed them down, no one saying a word. The only sounds were of dried oats and nuts being crunched between our teeth. There was a bit of chocolate flavor in my energy bar, and I nearly purred—it had been way too long since I'd eaten chocolate.

Isabel pulled out a canteen and passed it around. When my turn came, I tossed it back and drank deep of the water. It wasn't as cold as the stream, but it sure went down smooth. I wiped my mouth on my sleeve and handed it over to Isabel.

"Thanks," I said.

Isabel's green eyes lit up when she smiled. "You're quite welcome."

Dan stood patiently until everyone was finished eating the snack bars. He then shrugged his rucksack back onto his shoulders and nodded up the trail. "There's a shelter about two miles up ahead and we need to reach it before dark falls. We can't protect you all out here in the open."

Isabel nodded. "My flashlight batteries are dead, and you don't want to be walking around these mountains after dark with no light."

"We'll camp at the shelter tonight," Dan explained, "and then head for Ranger Station Tango at first light."

"What's that?" Jillian asked.

"What's what?" Dan asked.

"That Tango thing you mentioned," Jillian said.

Isabel waved her hand around. "We have dozens of ranger stations scattered around the Blue Summit Mountains and they're all named after the phonetic alphabet. As you might imagine, the higher up in the alphabet we go, the deeper in the mountains we go, so Tango's pretty far out in the sticks." Isabel turned to Dan. "How do we get the word out to the other searchers tonight?"

Dan shrugged. "I guess we'll have to wait until we get to Tango."

"It's a shame they have to endure another night worrying," Isabel said. "They've all been through enough."

"What're y'all talking about?" I asked.

"I lost my satellite phone before I met up with Dan, and the battery died on his, so we don't have radio contact with the rest of the search party." She frowned. "I just wish we could contact your parents and let them know you're all okay."

"My mom's here?" Charlie asked. "In Tennessee?"

"I haven't met her, but I heard she's been here all week." Isabel pointed toward me. "Your parents have also been here all week."

"How big is the search party?" I asked.

"About a hundred," Isabel said.

"Shouldn't we run into some of them?" I asked. "They might have a satellite phone."

Isabel shook her head. "Dan and I are long-shot searchers, walking backcountry trails where you all weren't likely to be. The search is being concentrated in the area surrounding where your truck was located, and we're about thirty miles from there." Isabel looked up at Dan. "Had you run into anyone else along the trail?"

"Only you." Dan glanced at my arm. "What happened to you?"

"Just a scratch. I fell in a river." I didn't want to say anything about the bear because I knew they would have to track it down and kill it, and that wasn't an option in my playbook. It was my fault for getting between the bear and food, and he was only doing what came natural.

Dan nodded at Isabel. "Want to take the lead? I'll bring up the rear."

Isabel nodded and stepped forward, heading up the narrow trail. "When we get to the shelter we'll cook up some beef stew for you guys," she called over her shoulder.

There was a low murmur of approval from the rest of us, and we stepped in line behind Isabel. I walked between Joy and Mable.

"What's the first thing you'll do when you get home?" I asked Mable.

"Catch up on *24*," Mable said. "That's the best television show ever. I can't wait to get the DVDs of the past few years, so I can catch up before the next season starts. Does it still start in November?"

I frowned. "I have some terrible news for you."

Mable's head jerked around, and she slowed so I could move beside her. "Don't tell me they killed off Jack Bauer."

"Worse. They cancelled the show in 2010."

"What? No way." Mable's face fell, and she walked in silence for a while.

Joy touched my shoulder. "What's the first thing you'll do?"

I glanced back at her. "Take you on a date—if you'll go with me."

Joy's smile drilled dimples into her rosy cheeks. "I would like that a lot. I want to eat at—"

"I wonder what else has changed since I've been gone." Mable shook her head. "I'm scared to go back, you guys. I don't know what's waiting for me back home. I mean, I didn't even finish middle school yet. What'll I do? Will I have to go back? If so, I'll be twenty-two or twenty-three before I can graduate. What if my parents are divorced? What if my grandpa's dead? He was really sick when I left, and I didn't get to spend much time with him. I'm terrified of what I'll find when I get back."

Joy rushed by me and wrapped her arm around Mable's shoulders. "It'll be okay. If you need anything at all you can always call me."

Mable looked at Joy, her eyes glistening. "I'd like that. I'll need to get your phone number and email address."

"Sure thing." Joy continued walking beside Mable. We must've walked several more miles when we started to slow down a bit.

"We're there," Ranger Isabel called from the front of the line.

When Joy, Mabel, and I caught up to Isabel, we came upon a large clearing with a log cabin situated in the center. The openings for the three windows and two doors were bare, but there was a roof and four solid walls. A dozen giant logs were situated around a fire pit and served as short stools.

"This is nice." Jillian had walked into the cabin and was leaning out one of the window openings.

Dan and Isabel tossed their rucksacks on the ground against the cabin and went to work on the fire pit. Isabel had a fire going in a jiffy, and Dan broke open four large cans of stew and poured them into a dented pot that appeared to have seen a lot of use.

While the girls explored the inside of the cabin, Charlie and I sat on two of the logs and watched the park rangers in action. They were as much at home in the forest as my mom was in her kitchen. Dan placed the pot on a metal grill suspended over the fire by several rocks, which made up the perimeter of the fire ring.

Before long, smoke was drifting from the pot and filling the air with the appetite-whetting aroma of beef, potato chunks, and carrots warming in brown gravy.

"It smells so good," Charlie said.

I nodded and studied the bandage on my forearm. It had been a while since I'd changed it. I pushed back the cloth and winced as it ripped free from my flesh.

"Are you okay?" Joy asked.

"I'll live." I looked over at the park rangers, who were at work on the food. "Hey, do y'all have a first aid kit I could borrow?"

Without looking up from where she was stirring the pot of stew, Isabel shot a thumb toward the rucksacks. "I've got a kit in my bag. Help yourself."

I stood, stretched, and ambled toward the cabin. It was right then that I realized how tired I was. I couldn't wait to eat and get some sleep. It would be our last night in the mountains, and I wasn't complaining. Just as I leaned for the rucksack, a twig snapped somewhere in the forest. I jerked upright and studied the forest surrounding the shelter. Was that Mr. Bush? I looked over at Dan and Isabel. They didn't seem bothered by the noise.

"Did y'all hear that?" I asked.

Isabel looked up, surveying the area. "It's probably a bear. I saw some scat as we walked up to the shelter. They won't bother us."

I nodded, reached for one of the rucksacks, and pushed the zipper open.

"Hey, that's my bag," Dan said.

I pulled open the flap and froze in place. The hair on the back of my neck stood straight and my heart stopped. Stuffed inside of Ranger Dan's rucksack were camouflage gloves, a piece of camouflage burlap with three slits in it, and a leafy suit.

CHAPTER 20

There was a gasp behind me, and I whirled around. Isabel had jumped to her feet and dumped the pot of stew onto the ground. Dan was standing across the fire from her with his revolver in his hand, pointed directly at her.

"What in God's name are you doing?" Isabel asked.

"It's him," I said. "He's the kidnapper...he's Mr. Bush!"

Isabel's brow furrowed. She stared from Dan to me, a quizzical look on her face. "What are you talking about?" She looked back at Dan. "Why are you pointing that gun at me? Stop playing around. Put it down...*now!*" Isabel pointed with her finger for emphasis.

Dan didn't say a word. He simply pulled the trigger. The revolver bucked in his hand, and Isabel grunted and leaned over. Screams sounded from inside the cabin, and the girls ran to the door just in time to see Isabel clutching at her stomach. She sank to the ground. Blood seeped through her fingers, dripping onto the ground in front of her.

I started to step forward, but Dan trained the handgun on me. "I need you, but I won't hesitate to kill you if I have to."

Joy gripped my arm, her nails digging into my flesh. The other girls were gasping behind me near the cabin, and one of them started to cry. With Dan's back turned to her, Isabel strained through the pain and moved a bloody hand from her stomach, quietly reaching for her gun.

"Why are you doing this?" I asked, trying to keep Dan focused on me, so Isabel could get her gun out and shoot him. "Just let us go, and we won't say a word. We'll just say we got lost and that we found our way out. No one needs to go to jail. Your secret's safe with us. I promise."

Charlie moved beside me, his fists clenched. "Abe, he can't get all of us. I think we should make a run for it. Whoever gets away can bring back the cops, the FBI, the army…everybody."

An evil grin played across Dan's mouth. "I like the courage. It'll be useful in the new world." He cocked the hammer on the revolver. "I can drop five of you faster than you can blink twice. Whoever I leave alive will be easy enough to corral."

"But I thought you said you needed us?" I asked.

"Everyone's replaceable." Dan pointed the gun at the girls and waved toward us with it. "Come stand by your boyfriends."

Jillian stood her ground at the corner of the cabin. "I'm not going back to that cave. I'd rather die."

Dan's eyes seemed to flash. He pointed the revolver toward Jennifer's head. "You just killed your friend—"

"No!" Jillian quickly moved next to Charlie and me. "Please don't kill her. I'm listening to you."

In my peripheral vision, I saw Isabel place her hand over her pistol. I cringed when she broke the snap on her holster. It sounded loud in the tense silence of the standoff. Dan appeared bored when he turned and put a bullet into Isabel's chest as she struggled to drag her pistol out of the holster. She collapsed backward and started gurgling. Dan fired a third shot that hit her in the face. Isabel tensed up and then her muscles relaxed. She lay still. Blood bubbled from her mouth.

Mable yelped and bolted for the forest. Charlie, Jillian, and Jennifer scattered in opposite directions. Joy hesitated, staring at me. Dan spun around. He snapped off gunshots in Charlie's direction. I pushed Joy to the ground and sprinted forward, making a beeline for Dan. When the third shot exploded, I heard Charlie scream. Dan then shoved the gun in my direction and pulled the trigger. I flinched, but the revolver clicked on a spent casing, and Dan growled. I was now within several feet of him, and he swung the revolver toward my head. I ducked under his arm and drove my right shoulder into his stomach. My momentum propelled him backward off his feet. I landed on top of him. The sprint had winded me, so I knew I had to finish him fast. But before I could pin him to the ground, Dan scrambled out from under me and bounced to his feet. The movement was nimble, and I stood cautiously. We circled each other. Charlie wailed in pain somewhere in the forest and I knew I had to drop Dan fast so I could tend to him.

Dan flashed that evil grin again. "I'm going to enjoy killing you two. Ever since you guys interrupted me taking your friend, things have been going south for me."

"Where's Brett?"

"You'll never know."

Although he had just got through killing another park ranger and shot Charlie, I felt uncomfortable squaring up against the law. What if I took him out? Would I go to jail? Would anyone believe our story that he was a rogue ranger? No matter. I now had to do what was necessary to survive. Never one to waste much time during a fight, I shot two quick jabs that connected with his face. Before the blood could drip from his nose, I pushed off with my right foot and smashed my right fist against his chin. His knees buckled and he stumbled back, but remained on his feet. Fear enveloped me. No one had ever remained standing after I'd landed that power shot. This guy had a granite chin.

Dan wiped the blood from his face and stared down at his hand. He opened his mouth to speak, but his words were cut short when a large tree branch crashed down on top of his head. Dried bark and splinters cascaded over him, and he dropped to his knees. It was then that I saw Joy standing behind him, her eyes wide and her face pale.

I sprung forward and kicked him square in the face with the sole of my right water shoe. He collapsed to his back on the ground, but rolled to his face and pushed off with his hands. Before he could regain his feet, I jumped on his back and wrapped my legs around his stomach and my left arm around his throat. Hooking my left hand in the crook of my right elbow, I grasped the left side of his head with my right hand and squeezed both arms as hard as I could. My left arm crushed his throat. He gasped for air and clutched at my arm. I felt the burn as his fingernails dug deep into my flesh. Somehow, he struggled to his feet and stumbled about, with me clinging to his back. He strained to force air into his lungs, and I strained to cave his windpipe in from the sides. In a surprising display of strength and will, Dan jumped up into the air and threw himself backward, landing hard on top of me. I grunted. Joy screamed. My grip loosened on his neck.

Dan jerked my arms free and rolled to his hands and knees. I tried to stand, but he grabbed my ankle with his vice grip and dragged my leg out from under me. I rolled to my back and kicked at his face with my other foot. It didn't seem to bother him as he lurched forward and punched down at my face. Blood sprayed down into my throat and I knew that my nose was broken—yet again. I lifted both arms to my face and deflected the blows that rained down on me.

Peeking through the slit between my arms, I waited until he lifted one of his arms to strike down at me again. When he did, I struck out, punching him as hard as I could in the throat. He gasped and clutched at the front of his neck. I reached up and shoved my left thumb in his eye, trying to touch the back of his head with it. He screamed in agony and began beating my left arm with his fists. I heard the crack of another tree limb and felt his body go limp.

My nose throbbed. My breath now came in labored gasps. Blood poured down from my nose, and I detected the metallic taste as it dripped into my mouth. With all of my remaining strength, I shoved Dan off me and onto his back, then crawled toward his head. Pushing one of his arms up above his head, I wrapped my right arm around his neck and arm and bore down as hard as I could, using my left hand to support my strangle hold. Through my blurred vision, I saw Joy on her knees, hitting Dan repeated in the chest with a large rock. She lifted it high over her head with both hands and then slammed it downward. She did it again and again. Her eyes were wild, her jaw set.

Dan struggled as I choked the life out of him and Joy beat him, but he finally lay still. Although he was limp, I held my grip, squeezing as hard as I could. Joy continued dropping the rock down on his chest, but the blows were coming in slow motion now as fatigue set in. I must've squeezed for a full two minutes and didn't let up until my arms started to fade. I turned Dan's neck loose and pushed him to the side, then rolled onto my back. I grunted as I tried to catch my breath. Joy fell beside me, equally tired. We lay there panting for several long moments. I could see the leaves swaying to and fro high above me and it made me dizzy. I had to close my eyes to calm the spinning.

Dry leaves rustled and twigs snapped as footsteps approached our position. I forced my eyes open. Jennifer ran up and dropped to her knees beside us. "Dear Lord, are you guys okay?"

I nodded and pointed toward the forest. "Charlie, go...go...check...on—"

Jennifer placed a finger over my lips. "Jillian's with him. She says he'll be fine. He's got an extra hole in his butt, but he'll be fine."

Joy was now sitting beside me, her wet hair plastered against her face and neck, her chest heaving.

"Deep breaths," I said. "In...in through your nose." I paused to take a deep breath myself. "And...out through your mouth. Slow and steady." I demonstrated—more for myself than for her—and felt my heartbeat starting to relax.

"Hey, look what I found." Mable had been digging in Dan's rucksack. She pulled out two satellite phones. "One's Isabel's and one's Dan's—and they both work!"

Jennifer walked over to her. "Call somebody."

"But who? I don't know the number to the police here."

"Call nine-one-one," Jennifer said.

Mable's eyes suddenly widened. "I'm calling my mom!"

Jennifer snatched up the first aid kit and one of the phones and they both hurried to Charlie and Jillian's location, each dialing numbers into the phones as they jogged into the forest. Joy stared longingly after them. I squeezed her hand. "Go with them. Call somebody."

She raised her eyebrows. "You sure?"

I smiled. "Your parents searched for weeks and believe you're dead. Don't make them wait."

Joy nodded and hurried off.

I closed my eyes and struggled to catch my breath. It took a while, but I slowly began to calm my panting. Off in the distance, I could hear the girls bawling amidst their excited chatter on the satellite phones. They were out of eyesight, but I could imagine the expressions on their faces and the shock on the other end of the phone. When I was able to move without feeling dizzy, I pulled myself to my knees beside Dan to feel for a pulse—first his wrist and then his neck. Nothing. I put my ear next to his lips. I couldn't feel anything. His skin was cool to the touch. His half-open eyes stared right at me. I waved my hand in front of his face. Not a blink of movement. He was dead. Really dead…and I'd killed him.

I turned quickly and stumbled toward a nearby tree and vomited. My legs shook. I felt cold. I wiped my mouth on my sleeve and wished for a bottle of mouthwash. I glanced around the camp area and realized I was all alone with two dead bodies. I pulled myself to my feet and hurried into the forest, following the sounds of the girls' voices. When I reached their location, Charlie was on the phone. I could tell he was talking to his mom. His eyes were red and so were the girls'. There wasn't a dry eye in the circle.

"I love you, too, Mom," Charlie said. "Yeah, I can't wait to see you."

Charlie pressed the "disconnect" button and looked up to hand me the phone. "It's your turn, big man."

I took the phone and stared at it for a long moment. I turned away, walked through the light underbrush and found a tree to sit against that was about twenty feet from the group. I dialed my mom's cell phone. She answered on the first ring.

"Abe? Is that you?" she asked.

"How'd you know?"

"Charlie just got off the phone with his mom. She's right here," Mom said. "We're all here—in the Blue Summit Mountains. We've been looking for y'all since Monday—right after they found Brett."

"What do you mean *found* Brett?" I asked.

"Oh my God—you haven't heard? You didn't know?"

"Didn't know what?"

"It's all over the news. That bad storm that blew through killed five people. They found Brett in a river... I'm so sorry, Abe. He didn't make it. He drowned." She broke down crying.

"He didn't drown," I said. "That crazy killer got him. Charlie and I saw him get taken."

"The doctors say he drowned in the storm," Mom explained.

It suddenly occurred to me—the chloroform rendered him helpless, so if Leaf Creature—Ranger Dan—threw him in the river, he would drown and no one would be the wiser. "You need to talk to the doctor—tell him he needs to check Brett for chloroform."

"Okay, Abe." Mom was bawling. "Here, talk to your dad."

I heard the phone change hands. "Abraham, are you okay?" It was my dad, and his voice cracked. I'd never heard him like that.

"I don't know, Dad." I bit back the tears. "I had to do something awful. I...I had to hurt someone really bad."

Silence on the other end. "What do you mean, Abe? What've you done?"

I wiped a tear that snuck from under my eyelid and leaked down my face. "The guy that kidnapped us... I had to..." I paused and took several breaths and blew them out to regain my composure. "I had to...I had no choice. Dad, he's not breathing and...and he doesn't have a pulse. He's dead. I mean...I...I killed that man, Dad. We were fighting, and I choked him out. I held it...I held the choke too long. He's...he stopped breathing. He's...um...dead."

"Now you listen to me, Abe." My dad's voice was soft, but confident. "You did what you had to do. Charlie told his mom that man shot him and the only reason he's still alive is because you tackled the bad guy. That man would've killed Charlie and all of y'all had you not done what you did. You saved everyone. You're a hero, son. And I'm very proud of you."

"But he's a park ranger—a cop. It's bad when you kill a cop."

"He was a dirty cop. You did what you had to do."

My jaw burned and I had to swallow several times so I could continue the conversation. "I didn't do it on my own. Joy helped me."

"Charlie told his mom y'all rescued those girls." Dad's voice trembled. "I can't say enough how proud I am of you. It scares me to think I almost didn't let you go."

"Thanks, Dad." I wiped my face. "I have to go. We need to figure out where we are so we can get out of here. I'll have to carry Charlie because he got shot in the—"

"No need to worry about that," Dad said. "Charlie described where y'all are and the rangers know the spot. There's a rescue helicopter en route to get y'all right now." There was some muffled talk in the background, and then Dad came back on. "The ranger who's with us said the helicopter should be there within a few minutes. He said there's a large meadow a hundred yards from the shelter. That's where they'll land the helicopter."

CHAPTER 21

I had just settled onto the doctor's stool when the door opened and a nurse walked in. She wore blue scrubs and her nametag said Buffy. She pointed me toward the examination table and said, "Jump up there, please."

It had been an hour since the helicopter had lifted us out of the mountains and transported us to the hospital in Knoxville. Charlie had been taken in first since his injury was the most severe and then the rest of us had been ushered to separate examination rooms. Still tired, I dragged myself off the stool and eased onto the white paper that covered the center of the table. It crumpled under me and I tried to fix it, but Buffy waved me off.

"Don't worry about that," she said. "It always slides off." She checked my blood pressure and then my heart rate. She held two fingers to my wrist and looked at her watch, frowning. "Do you exercise a lot?"

"Well, I've taken the last week or so off, but I usually work out every day."

She relaxed and nodded. "That explains it. Your pulse rate is forty-eight."

"Is that bad?" I asked. "Am I dying?"

Buffy laughed, then shook her head. "Normal is from sixty to a hundred beats per minute. The best I've seen was fifty-four beats and that was on a marathon runner, so you're in excellent shape. What do you do for exercise?"

"I box and dabble in mixed martial arts." I took two deep breaths so she could listen to my heart with her stethoscope and glanced at the clock on the wall. When I'd first arrived, a ranger told me Mom and Dad were on their way to the hospital with a police escort, so I figured they'd arrive at any minute.

Buffy then moved to the bandage on my arm and carefully removed it. She whistled when the partially healed gashes in my arm were exposed. "What on earth happened to you? Did that kidnapper do this?"

"No, ma'am," I said. "I was attacked by a bear."

Buffy gasped. "A real bear?"

"Nah, it was one of those wind-up deals from a gift shop in Gatlinburg."

First Buffy's eyes narrowed, then she smiled slightly. "You're a funny guy, aren't you?"

"I'm practicing my standup routine so—"

"Ma'am! Sir! You can't go in there!" hollered a voice from outside the room.

The door burst open, and my mom hurried in, followed closely by my dad. Startled and unsure of what was happening, I almost jumped back when Mom rushed in and threw her arms around me. She bawled loudly as she held me tight. I patted her back.

"It's okay, Mom," I said. "I'm fine."

After a long and uncomfortable moment, Mom backed away to look at me and her tear-streaked face turned pale when she saw my exposed arm. "Dear Lord, what on earth—"

"Rose," Dad said, "we need to give them some space. Let them do their job so they can make sure Abe's okay. We'll have plenty of time to visit with him later."

I nodded my thanks, and Dad gave me a wink before he led Mom out into the hallway. When the door was closed again, I shook my head and said, "Good grief."

Buffy turned to me and her eyes were moist.

"Not you, too?" I asked.

"It's just emotional." Buffy turned her head and fussed with my medical chart. "The entire city is celebrating. What you and your friend did was amazing. I don't blame your mom for being proud."

I laughed. "You know what we did? We got kidnapped. What's so special about that?"

"No, it's what you did after the kidnapping. You saved the lives of four very special young ladies, and you gave the families of those two boys closure. You might not think you're special, but I guarantee you those six families sure do!"

I scowled. "Well, a nice park ranger lady was killed today trying to help us, so I'm not in the mood to feel special."

Buffy turned back to my arm and began cleaning the wounds. After several minutes of silence, she said, "You really did a good job with these lacerations."

"It was Charlie. He took some first aid classes in high school, so I guess he knew what he was doing."

As Buffy was finishing up, the door opened again and a uniformed park ranger entered. He was holding a notebook. "Abraham Wilson?"

I nodded.

"I need to take your statement."

My heart definitely jumped a bit north of forty-eight. I just knew I was going to jail for murder. "Am I in some kind of trouble?"

"Well, that depends."

I gulped. "On what?"

"On what you tell me. I can't make an assessment until I hear what you have to say."

I nodded and sat up a little straighter.

The ranger turned to Buffy. "Can you leave us alone?"

She nodded, quietly left the room. The ranger pulled the doctor's stool in front of me and took a seat. He readied his pen over the pad and looked up. "Okay, start from the beginning and tell me how it was that you came into contact with the missing girls."

*   *   *

When I was done giving my statement, I spent some time with Mom and Dad—I had to answer a million questions—and then roamed the halls of the hospital until I located Charlie's room. Like me, the girls had been checked and released, but Charlie had been admitted for his gunshot wound. I found him alone in his hospital room.

"I guess you can take a double-barrel dump now, huh?"

Charlie started to laugh, then winced. "It hurts something fierce."

There were buttons on the side of Charlie's hospital bed, so I began pushing some of them. "What does this do?"

The bed started to incline; Charlie grabbed the side rail. "Whoa! Don't do that. You'll fold me in half."

I grabbed the doctor's stool and rolled it under me, then sat beside this bed. "Where's your mom?"

"She went get something to eat."

I sat quiet for a minute, then asked, "How're things between y'all?"

"Good. She wants me to come home."

"That's awesome," I said, "but what about her loser boyfriend?"

Charlie smiled. "He refused to come to Tennessee to look for us, so she dumped him."

"That's even better." I spun around on the stool, fingering the bandage on my right forearm. "So, are you taking your mom up on her offer?"

Charlie was thoughtful. "I think I'm staying."

I stopped abruptly in mid-spin. "Staying? What do you mean? Are you serious?"

"I think so. I spoke to one of the park rangers and he said I could become a forestry technician."

"A what?" I asked.

"I get to help clear trails, protect wilderness areas, maintain campgrounds—stuff like that." Charlie grinned. "I'm going to be a real mountain man, Abe."

"Don't you need a college degree for that?"

Charlie shook his head. "They said I can start at a GS-2 level, which requires high school only."

I nodded absently, processing this information and not liking it. "I don't know, Charlie. You really think you'd like doing that? I mean, you're a swamp rat. Guys like us are out of place in the mountains."

"You saw me out there, Abe. For the first time in my life, I feel like I really belong somewhere—and these guys genuinely want me to come to work for them." Charlie sat up in his bed. "We're heroes, Abe. We did something hundreds of park rangers and volunteers couldn't do—we rescued people who were missing for years! No one could solve the mystery, but *we* did! We're famous around here."

I stood and walked to the window to glance outside. The parking lot was aglow with spotlights and cameras. "There's a mob of reporters out there waiting to talk to us. They got my dad's number somehow and they've been calling all evening."

"Did you talk to anyone yet?"

I shook my head, as I turned from the window. "I don't want to. I'd rather just go back home and live in peace."

Charlie laughed. "Sorry, but that won't happen. They're going to hunt you down until they get an interview. We're paparazzi food now, my friend!"

I sat back on the stool, restless. "If you stay here, we'll never get to hang out."

"You can come up here during the summer and on spring break."

"I guess so," I said.

Charlie whistled. "You'll have one hell of a story to tell the girls at college."

I shook my head. "I plan on keeping a low profile, fly under the radar. Besides, I want to keep seeing Joy."

"What? I thought you were done with her."

"You know what the old folks say, 'You don't know what you've got 'til it's gone.'"

"Whatever, dude. If I were going to college, I'd live a single life—have *lots* of girlfriends."

"There you are," a voice called from behind me.

I turned and saw Joy standing in the doorway. She wore a light green sun dress and tan sandals. My jaw must've been dragging on the floor because her usually pale complexion was red. She quickly ran up to me and wrapped her arms around my neck, held me tight. I squeezed her back.

"Thank you so much for coming for me," she whispered in my ear.

A chill reverberated up and down my spine as her soft breath tickled my ear when she spoke. We held each other for what seemed like a small piece of eternity. We only released each other when Mable came into the room and plopped down at the edge of Charlie's bed.

"How's it going, Charlie?" Mable asked cheerfully.

"I've been better," Charlie said.

Joy and I moved beside her, and I asked, "Did you find out anything new?"

Mable nodded. "They said Mr. Bush kidnapped us to repopulate the earth—*Gross!*—because he thought the world would be destroyed on December twenty-first of last year. Can you believe someone could be so stupid?"

"He must've freaked when he woke up on December twenty-second and the world was still here," I said. "He probably didn't know what to do with y'all." A thought suddenly occurred to me. "If the world was going to come to an end up here, why didn't he sleep downstairs, too?"

"You know," Mable said, "I do remember him sleeping underground once. He seemed real anxious that night. He kept going up the ladder and peeking out the hatch. We didn't know what was up. That must've been the night of the twenty-first. Anyway, they said all the disappearances happened within five miles of Ranger Station Whiskey—"

"That cabin was a ranger station?" Charlie asked. "We were under a ranger station?"

"Yep," Mable said, "and Dan was in charge of it. In fact, he supervised all the searches in that area, which was why we were never found."

I scowled. "You'd think the park rangers would've suspected something when all of y'all were going missing in Dan's area and y'all were never found."

"More than thirty people go missing every year in Dan's territory," Mable said. "And they've all been found except for the six of us. So, when you break it down, only six out of more than two hundred people were never found, so those odds are pretty good and it wasn't enough to arouse any suspicion."

"What about the other ranger locations?" Charlie asked.

"They all have their fair share of missing hikers and campers," Mable said, "but they're all found—some dead, but most of them alive. When you consider the rangers rescue over a hundred people each year throughout the Blue Summit Mountains, it's easy to see how six disappearances over six years might go unnoticed."

"That makes sense," I said.

Mable lifted a finger. "Oh, and they said Ranger Dan must've been stalking you guys since the trailhead because there were a couple of rangers talking to him the morning you guys got here and they saw you tear down the posters."

"That was him?" Charlie asked. "I saw them watching us. I told you not to take those posters, Abe!"

Joy wrapped a hand around my waist and pulled herself close to me. "I'm sure glad you did."

We walked outside and left Mable and Charlie alone. When we were in the hall, Joy sat in a chair and hung her head. "Can I ask you something?"

I sat beside her. "Shoot."

"Now that we've been rescued, is it…"

I cocked my head sideways. "Is it *what?*"

When she looked up, I could read the pain in her eyes. "Is it over again…between us? Is it over?"

I swallowed the lump in my throat, twisted in my seat and squeezed her hard. I felt her gasp, but she didn't complain. "No. It's not over. I don't ever want it to be—"

"Excuse me," a booming voice called. "I need to speak with Abraham Wilson."

We turned to see a large man clad in a spiffy park ranger uniform. He had some stars on his shoulder and walked with an air of authority. I gulped as I felt my freedom pass before my eyes. I just knew this was the guy who was going to tell me I was going to prison for murder. After all, I had earlier confessed to murdering a park ranger, and I couldn't image the other park rangers thought it was funny. I'd always heard that cops didn't like it when one of their own got killed, and I'd just killed one.

I tried to control my voice, but even I could hear it crack. "That's me. I'm Abraham Wilson."

"I'm Major Dexter," the ranger said. "I read over your official statement. Do you stand by what you said?"

I nodded slowly. "It was all true, if that's what you're asking."

"We've been able to verify most everything you said and your statement led us to some disturbing files under Whiskey Station." Major Dexter nodded his head toward where Mable was still talking to Charlie. "The only reason she and her girlfriends are still alive is because the *doomsday* folks modified their prediction about when the earth would come to an end, so Dan thought he'd still need them. Otherwise, Dan planned to kill them and destroy any evidence of their existence."

Joy gasped. "He was going to kill all of us?"

"If the next date had come and gone and the world had not been destroyed, I'm afraid so." Major Dexter nodded toward Joy. "It appears the reason he kidnapped you was to replace a Katherine Turner who committed suicide."

Joy shuddered.

"It seems Dan was planning to use your friend Brett to replace one of the boys who died, but you guys interrupted him. No one has ever interrupted him before. It threw him off his game. It looks like he abandoned Brett's body to chase after you—we found bullet holes in some of the trees in the area—and the river rose and washed Brett's unconscious body away." Major Dexter frowned. "I'm really sorry about your friend. And unfortunately, we'll have to rule his death an accident."

"An accident?" I wanted to jump up out of my chair, but I thought better of it.

"I'm sorry, but yes."

I leaned over, rested my elbows on my knees. "How did y'all not suspect him? How could he be a park ranger and a kidnapper? How could you not know this guy who worked for you was doing this?"

Major Dexter sighed. "We cover a lot of territory. Most of our backcountry rangers live at their respective stations and only come out once in a while to get more supplies, so it's easy for someone like Dan to abuse his duties."

I smirked. "That's a bit mild—*abusing his duties.*"

"Son, I understand you're upset, and you have every right to be. I take full responsibility for what my people do and I've failed you, your friends, and the community. I can assure you I will make a public apology to you, personally, and to everyone whose lives have been impacted by what Dan did."

I took a deep breath and exhaled. "So, does this mean I'm not going to jail?"

"Of course not. What you did was heroic. You and your friend are to be commended for your actions."

"Well...wow...thank you," I said.

"Anyway," Major Dexter began, "after your story broke on the news, we were contacted by national parks across the country and it seems they've had unsolved disappearances similar to the ones we've had here. Thanks to you guys, we've been able to make a connection."

"You mean there are more people like Dan out there doing this?" I asked.

The major nodded, hesitated. "There's something else."

"What's that?" I asked.

"We went back to the shelter and found Isabel. Just like you said, she'd been shot to death. We also found signs of an intense struggle and blood all over the place, which supports your statement and the statement of your friends." Major Dexter took a deep breath, exhaled. "There's only one problem."

Joy and I were at the edges of our seats. "What is it?" we asked in unison.

"We couldn't find Dan Weathers anywhere. His body's gone."

BJ BOURG

 BJ Bourg is a former professional boxer and a lifelong martial artist who hails from the swamps of Louisiana. A thirty-year veteran of law enforcement, he has worked as a patrol cop, a detective sergeant, a police academy instructor, and the chief investigator for a DA's office. He has successfully investigated all types of felony cases and has trained hundreds of law enforcement officers in self-defense, firearms, and criminal operations. He retired in October of 2020 to pursue his boyhood dream of becoming a fulltime writer.

Throughout his career, Bourg has served on many specialized units such as SWAT, the Explosives Search Team, and the Homicide Response Team. He founded his agency's sniper program and served as its leader for nearly a decade. A graduate of seven basic and advanced sniper schools, he deployed as the primary sniper on dozens of call-outs, including barricaded subjects, hostage rescue operations, and fugitive apprehensions. He also served as the sniper instructor for the 2001 Louisiana Tactical Police Officers Association's Conference.

Bourg has been the recipient of numerous awards, including Top Shooter at an FBI Sniper School, the Distinguished Service Medal, and Certificates of Commendation for his work as a homicide detective. He is a public speaker and has also written dozens of articles for law enforcement magazines, covering a wide range of topics such as defensive tactics, sniper deployment, suspect interrogation, report writing, and more. Above all else, he is a father and a husband, and the highlight of his life is spending time with his beautiful wife and wonderful children.

Nowadays, he splits his time between Lafourche Parish, Louisiana and Tellico Plains, Tennessee while working on his next novel—whatever it might be.

Made in the USA
Columbia, SC
30 August 2022